# One
## Unforgettable
# Kiss

# A.C. Arthur

**HARLEQUIN**® KIMANI™ ROMANCE

If you purchased this book without a cover you should be aware that this book is stolen property. It was reported as "unsold and destroyed" to the publisher and neither the author nor the publisher has received any payment for this "stripped book."

| London Borough of Hackney | |
|---|---|
| 91300001061685 | |
| Askews & Holts | |
| AF | £6.50 |
| Recycling programs for this product may not exist in your area. | 5716687 |

ISBN-13: 978-1-335-21664-9

One Unforgettable Kiss

Copyright © 2018 by Artist Arthur

All rights reserved. The reproduction, transmission or utilization of this work in whole or in part in any form by any electronic, mechanical or other means, now known or hereafter invented, including xerography, photocopying and recording, or in any information storage or retrieval system, is forbidden without written permission. For permission please contact Harlequin Kimani, 22 Adelaide St. West, 40th Floor, Toronto, Ontario M5H 4E3, Canada.

This is a work of fiction. Names, characters, places and incidents are either the product of the author's imagination or are used fictitiously, and any resemblance to actual persons, living or dead, business establishments, events or locales is entirely coincidental.

® and TM are trademarks of Harlequin Enterprises Limited or its corporate affiliates. Trademarks indicated with ® are registered in the United States Patent and Trademark Office, the Canadian Intellectual Property Office and in other countries.

For questions and comments about the quality of this book please contact us at CustomerService@Harlequin.com.

**HARLEQUIN®**
www.Harlequin.com

Printed in U.S.A.

She looked so small under the thirty-foot-high—minimum—roof and rafters. But he now knew that she was fierce and determined. She was also the sexiest woman he'd ever seen.

"I know we haven't been on a real date," he said as he closed the distance between them. "But that doesn't mean a damn thing."

She was standing with her arms at her sides, the tips of her fingers barely reaching the hem of that sexy little black dress. There were red roses on the dress as well—one at her left shoulder, and the other on the right side of the skirt. She reached up and pushed her hair back from her face, tucking the curled strands behind her ears.

"I'm not sure I know what any of this means," she stated quietly.

"I want you, Harper," Garrek said. "I don't know why, because that's not what I came here for. I just know that since that first night when I saw you standing on that stage, I've been drawn to you. I can't seem to keep my hands off you."

With those words he lifted his hand, tracing his fingers along the line of her jaw.

D

LB of Hackney

05/18

913300001061685

Dear Reader,

I'm so excited to be back in Temptation! This time it's to see Garrek Taylor find his happily-ever-after.

Although, like his siblings, Garrek doesn't know he's looking for happiness when he comes back to his hometown, he finds it not long after he arrives. The independent and defensive Harper Presley was just the woman to break through Garrek's determined exterior. I love this couple because they both believed they knew what was best for their lives and their future, without even considering that the answer might actually mean they should be together.

The citizens of Temptation are also back and nosier than ever as they wait to see if yet another Taylor finds love in their tight-knit town. I am so in love with this series and these families. I cannot wait for you to visit with them and fall in love one more time.

Happy reading,

*A.C.*

**A.C. Arthur** is an award-winning author who lives in Baltimore, Maryland, with her husband and three children. An active imagination and a love for reading encouraged her to begin writing in high school, and she hasn't stopped since.

## Books by A.C. Arthur

### Harlequin Kimani Romance

*Defying Desire*
*Full House Seduction*
*Summer Heat*
*Sing Your Pleasure*
*Touch of Fate*
*Winter Kisses*
*Desire a Donovan*
*Surrender to a Donovan*
*Decadent Dreams*
*Eve of Passion*
*One Mistletoe Wish*
*To Marry a Prince*
*Loving the Princess*
*Prince Ever After*
*One Unforgettable Kiss*

Visit the Author Profile page
at Harlequin.com for more titles.

# Chapter 1

"We have another bid! Going once. Going twice. Going…three times, and it's gone! Sir, you're our lucky winner!"

Garrek heard the applause behind him and turned to see what was going on. The room wasn't large—it included a dance floor in the center and a homemade bar setup in the corner, where he'd quickly found a seat. But Garrek was not comfortable at this moment, as he noticed the gaze of every person in the room was now on him.

"Come on up here and claim your prize!" a short man with his hair parted and gelled down to the side announced into the microphone he was holding.

The crowd clapped and cheered, stepping aside until a walkway had been formed, starting where Garrek sat at the bar and ending at the two steps that led to the stage.

"Come on. Don't be shy. Your prize is waiting!" the man continued.

Garrek had no idea what he'd won, because he hadn't entered any contest. All he'd done was follow the crowd that had been heading into this old building because they'd looked excited about coming in here. And when he'd seen the sign on the door that read Cash Bar, Garrek had felt a wave of relief. He'd needed a drink. He didn't want one, because each time he swallowed his favorite rum, he remembered the night that he knew would haunt him for the rest of his life. But he needed it. That was a simple fact.

It had been a long week, one he was still wondering how he'd survived. His career was on the line, and after two Cuba libres, his mouth was still dry. He'd just held up his hand to signal the bartender when the man on the stage began to speak.

"He's a handsome one, too," a woman said. She had pushed through the crowd and stopped right in front of him. "Nice body and everything."

The last was said as she lifted small hands and pressed them firmly, front and center, on his chest.

"Harper, you let me know if you need any help with this one." The woman spoke over her shoulder, as her hands squeezed his pectorals.

Garrek was wearing a white T-shirt that fit him snugly, a fact that the woman who looked to be in her midsixties seemed to enjoy.

"I'm Connie, and I'd be happy to escort your fine self up to the stage."

Before Garrek could decline her offer, Connie, with her cap of silver hair and no more than five-foot stature, was right beside him, lacing her arm through his and holding on tight. She wore a pale-green-and-white polka-dot dress, and a huge white flower was pinned close to her left shoulder. Her grin was wide as she looked up at Garrek, and when he continued to stare down at her, she winked.

Before Garrek could react, she was taking a step, and he found himself quickly slipping off the wobbly stool he'd been perched on to follow her lead. They moved down the path that reminded Garrek of the old *Soul Train* line, sans music. He hadn't purchased anything but drinks since he'd arrived not even a half hour ago, so he doubted he'd won a raffle.

The people on the outskirts clapped as they walked by, and Connie nodded as if she were in her element being the center of attention. When they came to the two steps that led up onto the stage, Garrek had to hold Connie steady as her knees wobbled with each step up. A quick flash of memory had him thinking back to his late teenage years in Pensacola, the years when his mother's condition was getting worse.

"Here we go," the man said as he touched the younger woman standing next to him on the shoulder. "Now, you can thank us later, Harper. But this is what the lovely ladies of the Magnolia Guild wanted to give to you."

She looked frightened.

That's the first thought that came to Garrek's mind as he gazed at the young woman standing next to the other man, who was doing all the talking.

Garrek was a navy pilot, but he'd been trained as a pilot first. His instinct to protect was strong and quick.

"That's right, Beuford," Connie said as she stepped away from Garrek to grab the microphone from the man's hand.

Beuford frowned down at her, but Connie didn't notice, because she'd already turned her attention to the other woman.

"Now, Harper, us ladies at the guild have known you since you were a little thing running around town with scraped knees and dirt smudges on your face. Haven't we, ladies?" Connie asked and looked out to the crowd.

A group of six women wearing the same white corsage as Connie stood close to the stage, nodding their agreement.

"So don't be shy. We had this auction just for you 'cause we knew we'd get you a good man that way. Good men always step up to the plate," Connie continued.

The woman—the one Connie had called Harper— didn't move. She was wearing a long black-and-white skirt and a sleeveless white blouse. Her hair was pulled back from her face, so Garrek couldn't tell how long it was.

"You were the highest bidder, coming in at two thousand twenty-five dollars," Beuford said, stepping around to clap a hand on Garrek's shoulder.

"Woo-wee, over two thousand dollars for a date with our little Harper!" Connie yelled.

She grabbed Harper by the hand and pulled her closer to where Garrek stood, shocked speechless by what was happening. He'd been in Temptation for a little over an hour, and already he was the center of attention. Again.

To be fair, he was sharing the attention with the strangely quiet Harper, just as years ago he'd shared the spotlight with his five siblings. Wait, had they just said he was the highest bidder? Meaning he was paying for a date?

The thought was almost laughable, because the last

thing in this world Garrek wanted right now was a date, and he certainly wouldn't be paying for one if he did. Clapping resumed, and music started to play as Connie pushed Harper's hand into Garrek's. He'd be lying if he said he didn't feel the little spike of heat at the contact. But he instantly brushed it aside. Garrek had grown really good at ignoring things he didn't want to deal with.

"Well, say something, Harper," Connie insisted and put the microphone in front of the woman.

Without thinking twice, Garrek took the microphone and spoke into it. "Harper and I want to thank you for coming out tonight. We'd also like to announce that the money raised here tonight will be donated to—" He paused.

Then he looked over to Harper. Garrek was six feet even. Harper was a tall woman, her shoulder only a couple inches shorter than his.

"The Veterans Fund," she said after staring at him questioningly for a few seconds. "The two thousand and twenty-five dollars will go to Temptation's Veterans Fund and provide support for those who fought hard to protect us and this country."

Garrek's first thought was, how had she known who he was?

Connie snatched the microphone at that point. "No. No. That's not the plan for the money. It's going to the Guild, because we planned this little event. We're getting a sign to hang over the doorway to our headquarters. It'll be real classy, and that way everyone will know where to find us."

Connie nodded as she spoke, as if everyone was naturally going to agree with her. The six women whom Garrek suspected were also from the Guild mimicked

Connie's movements, and there were some murmurs from the crowd that said they were confused. Well, they could join the club, Garrek thought.

Then he spoke again, without the need for a microphone. He was loud enough that they could hear him across the room where the bar was. He knew this by the shocked look he received from the bartender after he announced, "My check will be written to the Veterans Fund. Any other proceeds from this event can be used for whatever purpose the Guild decides."

Connie gasped and clamped her thin lips closed, her facial expression clearly annoyed. Garrek doubted she was thinking about touching his pecs again at this moment. Beuford looked from Garrek to Connie and back to Garrek again without saying a word. The once-clapping crowd had now fallen quiet, some of them with mouths open in surprise, others whispering to the person next to them. All of them staring at Garrek.

How the hell had this happened?

He'd come here to get away from people looking at him in question. Now, it seemed he'd walked right into yet another sticky situation with a woman. He wanted to curse, or possibly even run as far from this place as he'd just run from Washington. Instead, Garrek made his way off the stage, slowly pulling the woman named Harper along with him.

Harper was done!

The only reason she'd put on a skirt and come to the Sadie Hawkins dance was for business. What better way to promote Presley Construction—a company owned and operated by a woman—than to come to a dance where the women were supposedly liberated enough to ask the men out? Yet these same women apparently thought Harper needed help finding a man, when the truth was Harper wasn't even sure she ever wanted a man permanently in her life. She certainly wasn't on a personal crusade to find one who would take precedence over everything else in her life.

Coming here tonight had seemed like a good idea when she'd first thought of it. This dance was an annual event, like so many others in Temptation. Up until tonight, it had been one that Harper had proudly stated she'd never attended.

She shouldn't have broken the streak.

If she'd known what the Magnolia Guild had secretly planned for tonight, she wouldn't have come. In fact, she might have left town completely. How embarrassing. How totally and utterly humiliating, to stand on that stage and be auctioned off like cattle. But she'd been trapped. Running off the stage and out of the hall would have definitely made her the butt of the whole town's jokes for the foreseeable future. Forget trying to get anyone to hire her to do construction work—they'd be too busy laughing at poor little Harper who'd had to be auctioned off to a man instead of being able to get a date on her own.

So she'd stood there, frozen to that spot, staring at one of the columns in the center of the room that had been wrapped in pink and blue streamers. Everyone was staring at her, she knew. They were talking about her again. Some things never changed, especially not in Temptation.

"Who will bid two hundred and fifty dollars to take Harper out on a date?" Beuford Danforth had asked after Connie had not very politely dragged Harper onto the stage.

Beuford was the unofficial host of just about every event in Temptation, since he'd been a radio personality for twenty-five years before retiring. When there wasn't some type of town get-together, Beuford could be found on the wraparound front porch of his lime green–shingled house, putting together one of his Lego creations. He was seventy-two years old and still fascinated with the toys.

Harper's cheeks had burned, not only at the question, but at the complete and utter silence that fell over the room like a tent. She'd clasped her hands in front of her and clenched her fingers until she worried she might actually pull off skin. Her heart beat wildly and her shoulders had begun to shake.

All reactions she'd had before and ones she'd sworn she would never have again.

She'd tuned out everything by that point—everything except the man touching her hand. At that moment a jolt brought her back to reality, and she'd looked up into warm brown eyes. He wasn't from Temptation; that was her first coherent thought as he held her hand tightly in his. There was no man in Temptation who looked like this. Harper would remember if there was.

He was taller than her, with an athletic build—a very toned and alluring athletic build. His hands were large and engulfed her long fingers. His light complexion was a perfect backdrop to the dark hair of his goatee and thick eyebrows. He was wearing simple dark slacks and a white T-shirt, yet he still managed to look like a movie star—perfect enough to be on the big screen seducing women across the world.

Women like her.

No, never her, she'd reminded herself just in time to reply to the question he'd asked.

"The Veterans Fund," she'd said after taking what she hoped was a mind-clearing deep breath and releasing it. "The two thousand and twenty-five dollars will go to Temptation's Veterans Fund and provide support for those who fought hard to protect us and this country."

Her grandfather and her father and all the other brave men like them.

Connie hadn't liked that one bit, a fact Harper knew she'd hear about in town for the next week. When Constance Gensen was upset, everyone in Temptation heard about it. This time, as was the case too often in the past, Harper would be involuntarily entrenched in Connie's discontent.

"Do you need a ride home?"

His voice was deep and had the effect of a good shot of whiskey—grabbing her immediate attention and making her shiver all over.

"Ah, no," Harper replied and then cleared her throat. "I drove my car."

"Because you didn't have a date."

"I didn't need one," she replied quickly and with certainty.

"Yeah, I know how that feels," he said and then looked away.

"You're not from around here," Harper stated. "Are you visiting someone?"

He didn't reply, but he did look at her again. Then, as if just remembering, he looked down at her hand. The one he was still holding. Harper's cheeks warmed again and she attempted to pull away, but he held tight.

The Freedom Hall—now called the Gloria Ramsey Place—was part of the old shoe warehouse that had gone out of business ten years ago. The building had been purchased by Kittinger Hale, a retired schoolteacher who had hit the lottery and found his birth mother in the same week. Gloria Ramsey had been on the run from her abusive husband when she'd stopped in Temptation to give birth to the son she would leave at All Saints Hospital the next morning. Buying the building and slapping Gloria's name across the front window was—Harper figured—Kittinger's tribute to Gloria. To the citizens of Temptation, it hadn't meant nearly as much. The building would always be called the Freedom Hall, after Freedom-brand shoes, which had been manufactured there for fifty years before the company went out of business.

The building was on the corner of Maple and Grove Streets. There was a black streetlamp still sporting the multicolored spring fling banner just a few feet away from them. The light was excruciatingly bright, bringing even more attention to the fact that they were holding hands.

"I shouldn't be here," he said. Harper stopped looking around to see if anyone was outside at the moment, and stared at him.

"Neither should I," she replied.

He was rubbing his thumb over the back of her hand at this moment. Attempting to pull away again was certainly an option, except that Harper didn't want to break the contact. The warmth from his hand was comforting, his strong grip protective and the heated spikes moving quickly throughout her body foreign, but not unpleasant.

"I should go," he said.

"Me too," she replied.

Yet neither of them moved.

There was space between them, even though their hands were connected. His body wasn't touching hers, and while she felt as if she were being physically drawn to him, Harper hadn't moved an inch.

So why did it suddenly seem warmer?

"Thanks for agreeing to donate to the veterans," she said because she didn't know what else to say.

"It's no problem," he replied.

Then, finally, after more silent moments, Harper figured this situation was absolutely ridiculous. She yanked her hand away from his—not realizing he'd lightened his grip so that her extra effort made her look even more preposterous.

"I'll also apologize for what just happened back there. I don't know what they were thinking, but getting a tourist roped into their shenanigans probably wasn't the plan."

"I'm not a tourist," he told her in a very exacting way. He didn't sound like he was offended, but that he wanted her to know this for certain. It was odd, but then, wasn't this entire situation?

"Fine. Well, I apologize. Good night."

"I'll walk you to your car."

"It's not—" Her words trailed off as he once again took her hand.

"Which way?" he asked.

"Down here on the corner," she replied.

Now she was walking down the street with a guy she didn't know. This was strange. And it was dangerous. And she should know better.

"Well, good night, again," Harper said when they

reached the car. She kept her back to the driver's door and her eyes on him.

He was standing with his legs slightly spread, hands tucked into the front pockets of his slacks. Again, Harper noted how attractive he was and how that thought exacerbated the unsettled feeling in the pit of her stomach.

"Good night, Harper," he said.

Once again neither of them moved.

It was confusing, because just fifteen minutes ago Harper had wanted nothing more than to run out of the hall and to her car. She lived on her grandfather's farm, on the outskirts of town about twenty minutes from the hall. Tonight was Sunday, which meant that Pops and her dad were sitting in front of the television watching whatever sport they could find. Uncle Giff and Aunt Laura would be at their house a little closer to town, probably sitting in front of their television, too. There wasn't much else to do in Temptation on a Sunday night, except maybe stand around with a strange—yet undoubtedly sexy—guy.

He came straight toward her, stopping only a breath away. A breath that Harper immediately sucked in when he closed his eyes and shook his head. Before Harper could make another move, he was gone. He moved even faster than he had before, because by the time Harper found her breath and let it out slowly, a hand going to her thumping heart, he had disappeared around a corner.

What the hell had just happened?

Harper had no clue. What she did know was that she wasn't going to forget her first and only Sadie Hawkins dance, or the undeniable arousal that her highest bidder had awakened.

## Chapter 2

He was undressing in front of her. Slowly unbuttoning the three buttons at the top of his shirt before pulling it up and over his head. His body was magnificent—bulging muscles, ripped abs, narrow waist. It was like a *Playgirl* centerfold.

When his strong fingers touched the button of his pants, Harper sucked in a breath. He was actually getting naked. The tightening of her nipples at that thought drew her gaze down her own body. She was already naked. Lying on her bed, legs spread wide in open invitation.

Had she invited him to her place? Her room? Her...

He stepped closer to the bed now, his pants unbuttoned, his chest bare. His gaze was hot, sending heated glares down her body until every inch of her exposed skin felt as if it were on fire.

"Show me what you want," he said, his voice thick with desire. "Show me how to please you, Harper."

What?

No, she couldn't.

It was wrong. Wasn't it?

She lay back against the pillows then, heart beating wildly as her throat tightened and the heavy fog of anxiety began to settle in. She was a healthy twenty-nine-year-old woman who had a right to know what she wanted and to ask for it. No, to demand it. She deserved that, didn't she?

Especially after all that Harper had been through, all the humiliation and embarrassment she'd endured over the years. And not just in Temptation, but even during the four years she'd spent in Virginia. She'd been a trouper, as her father would have said. She'd stood strong in the face of adversity each and every time.

So, yes, dammit, she deserved something for herself. For once in her life, she deserved pleasure that she so often dreamed of. And tonight, she was going to take it.

With that resolution in mind, Harper opened her mouth to speak. She let one hand fall down to cup her breast while the other moved farther down to rest on her cleanly shaved mound. She was going to show and tell him what she wanted. He'd bid and donated a good chunk of money on her behalf tonight, and he wanted her. She wanted him, too, so much that she was ready to take the biggest risk of her life. She was about to invite him to make her…

Harper's eyes popped open at that moment. She sat straight up in her bed. Her bedroom was empty, but her heart was still beating fast, and between her legs moisture still pooled as a reminder of her arousal. But he wasn't there. She'd been dreaming about a man she didn't even know. Fantasizing about someone she would never have.

Some things never changed.

"I told Mama it wasn't going to work. You're just not interested in men. Don't know why you're still trying to keep that a secret."

Harper picked up the to-go cup of coffee and considered tossing the hot liquid into Leah Gensen's perfectly pretty face. Then Harper thought better of that act, knowing it would draw too much attention to them. Ignoring Leah's snide comment was the next option. Harper had made a habit of doing just that since she and Leah were in second grade. But Harper wasn't seven years old anymore, and she couldn't help it if Leah hadn't figured that out yet.

"No secrets to be kept," Harper said as she used her free hand to retrieve three dollars from the back pocket of her jeans. "But the next time your mother wants to play matchmaker, she should take note of the fact that you're available. Especially since your third divorce was finalized last month."

Leah's pert, glossy, red-painted lips turned upward into a smirk as she narrowed her gaze at Harper.

"At least I've had a man," Leah snapped.

"And I've got a college degree and own a business, while you're serving coffee at your aunt's coffee shop. You want to continue keeping score of who's doing what, go right ahead, but I've got work to do."

Harper dropped the money for her daily large coffee and plain bagel on the counter and turned to leave.

"That's my girl," Smitty Hallern said as Harper passed the table near the front window where he always sat.

"Hi, Mr. Hallern," Harper said after mustering a smile.

Smitty played poker with Harper's grandfather on Saturday nights. He had enlisted in the army the same time as her grandfather but had received a medical discharge when he'd suffered a severe asthma attack.

"Don't let 'em get to you today," Smitty said with a nod toward the front counter, where Leah and the other customers stood. "They always need something or somebody to talk about. Tomorrow they'll be on to a different story."

Harper shrugged. "It's their life. They can live it how they please."

It was an awful life, Harper thought—sitting around a café all day talking about people and what they did or didn't like about them. Pitiful, really.

"That's true," Smitty continued. "But it ain't good for you or people like you to hear all that negative talk. That's what happened to Teddy and Olivia's marriage. People kept talking about them and what they were doing with those TV folks. It got right messy around here with the rumors flying around. People got hurt, and then Olivia packed her kids up and left."

Smitty went off on tangents often. Normally, it was something about the "good ol' days," as he and her grandfather called them. To which Harper would simply listen and smile. It was nice to hear their memories, and sometimes she even managed to learn a little about how the world was sixty years ago.

This morning, however, she had a headache. She'd been up for hours already, after waking from the disturbing dream. She was tired and cranky, and Leah hadn't helped the situation at all.

"Right, I'll keep that in mind, Mr. Hallern," she said and pressed her back to the front door of the shop.

"Yeah, gossip can cause lots of pain," he continued with a nod. There was a newspaper spread out on the table in front of him, a half-full cup of coffee and crumbs from what looked like a muffin he'd already eaten on the small plate to his left. "But it looks like the kids are coming around," he said, rubbing a hand over the tight black-and-gray curls at his chin. "First the oldest boy came on home, and now I hear you ran into one of the other sons last night."

That caught Harper's full attention.

"Last night?" she asked. "Who did I run into last night?"

"Garrek Taylor. He's the one who placed the winning bid on you. At least that's the news going around this morning. Connie was in here about an hour ago whining about the check he wrote to the Veterans Fund instead of to her group of cackling hens."

He shook his head then, and Harper swallowed. Her throat was suddenly dry.

"That was Garrek Taylor?"

"Yep," Smitty said. "The navy pilot. Millie came in right behind Connie, and those two got to talking. Millie thinks she knows all there is to know about the Taylors. Probably 'cause she used to be spitting jealous of Olivia for marrying Teddy. Crazy, that's what womenfolk can be sometimes."

Harper was still trying to wrap her mind around what he'd just told her. Garrek Taylor, one of the infamous Taylor sextuplets, was back in Temptation. The story was that his mother had packed up her six children who were seven years old at the time, and moved to Florida. She'd left behind their family reality show and her cheating husband. Now, not only was Garrek the second of the Taylor sextuplets to return to town, but he'd bid on a date with her. He'd also invaded her dreams, bringing her to a fevered point she'd never been to before—in real life or a fantasy.

Could this week possibly get any worse?

"Welcome home!" Gray said the minute Garrek opened the door.

His older brother didn't wait for a return greeting or an invitation to come in, but instead pushed past Garrek until he was completely inside the little room Garrek had rented at the Sunnydale Bed-and-Breakfast.

It had been eight years since Garrek had seen Gray in person. The last time he'd actually laid eyes on his brother was via a Skype call, at the reading of their father's will, nine months ago.

"Hello, Gray," Garrek said as he closed the door and walked to where his brother stood next to a dark green sofa that faced the oak television stand.

He'd been up for the last hour reading and hadn't yet decided when he was going to pay his brother and his new family a visit. It seemed he no longer needed to contemplate that act.

"It's good to see you, man," Gray said and then stepped closer to pull Garrek into a hug.

Garrek and Gray were the same height, six feet even, but Gray had a broader frame and a penchant for expensive clothes, while Garrek was much more understated in his dark blue Levi's and black Maryland Terps T-shirt.

"It's good seeing you," Garrek admitted as they pulled apart. "Congratulations are in order."

Gray took a seat on the couch, and Garrek noted his brother wasn't wearing the tailored suits an international businessman, like him, would. Today he wore khaki pants, a white button-down Polo shirt and brown leather shoes that Garrek was certain had cost a small fortune. As the CEO of his own electronics company, Gray was a wealthy man. In fact, all of the Taylor sextuplets were wealthy, after Gray discovered the money their father had left them a few months ago.

"Marriage, new house and a baby on the way," Garrek continued. "Just like old times—Grayson Taylor does it big or he doesn't do it at all."

Gray smiled and Garrek chuckled as he sat on the other end of the couch. That was one of the things he admired most about his brother—his ability to get whatever it was he wanted done, and in grand fashion. Garrek was much too introverted to be the type of go-getter Gray was.

"Two babies on the way," Gray added. "You didn't get my last letter that said Morgan is carrying twins?"

Garrek shook his head. The letter was probably in the huge stack of mail he'd dumped into the bottom of his suitcase when he began packing for this trip. He'd taken some things out to read this morning, but it was information that Gray had sent him a while ago.

"Wow, twins!" Garrek stated and extended a hand to Gray. "Like I said, you always go big."

Gray accepted his brother's handshake and shrugged. "But I don't know that this was all on me. You know she already has a set of six-year-old twins."

"Right, Gemma told me about them. Jack and Lily, right?"

Gray nodded. "Yeah, they're the best things that have ever happened to me. All of them, and coming back here. I can't imagine my life without them now."

Garrek didn't know how those words made him feel.

Gray had always been about his business and traveling the country. He'd never planned to settle down beyond his penthouse in Miami and his always-fueled personal jet. Hearing him talk about this woman and these children who had somehow changed him amazed Garrek.

"So tell me what brings you here. And why didn't you call me to let me know you were coming? Morgan and I would have gotten a room ready for you at the house."

"Nah," Garrek told him with a shake of his head. "This was a last-minute decision, and I don't want to put you out in any way."

"Don't be silly, man. You're my brother—you couldn't put me out. Especially not in that big house. I know you remember there are five bedrooms in that place."

Garrek did remember. Gray was living in their childhood home on Peach Tree Lane.

"Yeah, I remember. But you've got your family there now. It's your house." Garrek leaned forward, resting his elbows on his knees, and shook his head, because he was still trying to grasp all the changes that had happened in the past few months. The ones with Gray and the other Taylor sextuplets, and the ones with him personally.

"You're welcome to stay there, but I'm not gonna push. Morgan will do enough of that when she sees you today. So come on—she was about to start cooking breakfast when I left the house. Her exact words were 'bring him home to eat with us.'"

"Ah, no. I'm just going to hang out here for a while and catch up on some reading. I'll try to stop by later or maybe tomorrow."

Gray shook his head. "Look, Garrek, I know how you like to stay to yourself. I remember we used to give you hell about that growing up. But I get it, you want your space. Joining the navy and flying planes gave you lots of distance from our family and all that came with it. Unfortunately, you're back in Temptation now. The place where there are no secrets, no privacy, and people who act like you're related even though there's no blood connection."

Garrek had known that when he came here. He'd known, and yet he hadn't thought to go anyplace else.

"I hadn't planned to stay long enough for anyone to even know I was here. I mean, I was gonna call you, of course. But I don't know anyone in this town, and they definitely don't know me."

"That's where you're wrong," Gray said as he stood. "It's almost ten a.m. By this time everybody in Temptation knows that Garrek Taylor is back in town."

Garrek stood, too, staring at Gray with confusion. "How would they know that? I just got here last night."

"And you paid twenty-five hundred dollars to take the town tomboy on a date. Bright and early this morning, that check you wrote landed on the desk of Shirley Hampstead, town comptroller, who plays bingo with Joya Martina, Georgia Sanford and Millie Randall. Millie's the director of Temptation's Chamber of Commerce, and her office is right down the hall from Shirley's. Joya volunteers at the hospital on Monday mornings, and after Shirley told Millie, Millie called Joya, who saw Wendy, Morgan's sister, in the hallway on her way to work and told her. Wendy called Morgan and now," he finished with a shrug and a smile, "I'm here to bring you back to the house for breakfast."

"Wow" was all Garrek could offer in response.

"Yep," Gray replied with a chuckle. "Welcome to Temptation!"

* * *

*Welcome to Temptation* was exactly what Garrek was thinking fifteen minutes later when he stepped onto the wraparound porch of the house on Peach Tree Lane.

He'd been looking around at the place that was obviously undergoing renovations when something to the right caught and held his attention. That something was perfectly shaped and tempting. His mouth had immediately watered at the sight, his body tensing. Of course, it wasn't the first time he'd glimpsed a female behind, and at thirty years old he was pretty sure it wouldn't be the last. But there was something about the way the worn denim outlined these particular curves.

She was bending over, counting slats of wood that had been piled toward the far end of the porch. And he was drawn to her. That's about all he could say to describe why he let Gray go on into the house while he walked closer to where she stood. There was a familiarity that Garrek attributed to the jolts of lust spearing quickly throughout his body. He hadn't come to this town to meet or sleep with another woman—in fact, that was the last thing he should be thinking of—yet he continued to walk until she stood up straight.

The long swaying end of sandy-brown hair pulled into a ponytail swished over the back of a light blue T-shirt that was tucked snugly into the waist of those enticing jeans. Garrek's breath caught seconds before she turned to face him because he knew…he didn't know how, but he did, and when her shocked expression met his and held, he acknowledged that he was in trouble.

Big, delectable trouble.

# Chapter 3

"Oh!"

Her lips formed a perfect O shape as she released the one syllable, her eyes growing wider.

*Cute.* That's the first word that came to Garrek's mind as he looked at her. She was cute. And cute normally wasn't his thing. Except when the sprinkle of brown freckles that marched boldly from one cheek across the bridge of her nose to the other cheek held his gaze. There were gold studs in her ears, and her eyes were a dark brown, which made an instant contrast to her cappuccino complexion.

"Good morning," he said when it seemed the silence between them was going to stretch too long.

"Mornin'," she replied and then tried to walk around him.

Their arms touched, skin to skin, and they both

looked down at the contact. She yanked her arm away first, rubbing her hand up and down the spot where they'd just touched.

"Well, I see you two have met. Again," a very cheerful voice said.

Garrek looked up to see a short and very pregnant woman making her way toward them. This had to be his sister-in-law. He smiled and extended his hand to her.

"You must be Morgan. I'm Garrek. It's really nice to meet you."

Once she was close enough, Morgan pushed Garrek's extended arm out of the way and stepped in, her arms going immediately around his waist. Garrek joined in the hug, which was tight on her part and cordial on his.

"We don't welcome family with a handshake around here," Morgan was saying as she pulled away.

Garrek smiled down at her. She had a friendly face and quick, assessing eyes. Without missing a beat, Morgan reached out and grabbed Harper's arm just as she was trying to slip away.

"Harper, I hear you and Garrek met last night at the dance. Have you decided where you're going on your date?" Morgan asked.

Garrek hadn't thought about the date he'd paid for, even though Harper's leery gaze had stuck with him throughout the night.

"I apologized for that already," Harper said. "I didn't know they were going to do it."

"Nonsense," Morgan said and let her hand slide down Harper's arm until she was lacing their fingers together. "I think you going out with Garrek is a great idea. You can show him around Temptation, since he's been away from town for a while."

"I didn't know he was your in-law, either." Harper shook her head. "I would never want things to be awkward. You know I'm serious about my business and trying to be professional, Morgan."

She continued to speak only to Morgan, not so much as glancing in Garrek's direction. He thought about that even as his fingers itched to move the strands of hair that had escaped her ponytail away from her face. It was a picture-perfect summer day in this quaint little town. He'd noted the colorful storefronts on Main Street leading the way to tree-lined streets, perfectly manicured sprawling lawns and large family homes on the ride over with Gray. It was exactly as he remembered from all those years ago. And Garrek had felt the same way he had back then—like he didn't belong.

"There's nothing wrong with having a social life," Morgan was saying when Garrek stopped his momentary trek down memory lane and gave his attention to their conversation once more.

The smile Harper offered Morgan was conciliatory and didn't touch her eyes.

"Let's start with breakfast," Morgan continued. "Coffee's hot, French toast is sweet and Gray's probably in there burning the eggs."

Garrek chuckled at that. "He never could cook eggs. That was always Gemma's specialty."

"That's exactly what he said," Morgan added. "Harper, won't you join us?"

She was already shaking her head. Garrek hadn't expected anything less.

"No, thanks," Harper said. "I have a lot to do this morning. Want to get the shiplap up in the den. Craig has Roy and Pete upstairs working double time on the nursery, per Gray's request. And Marlon's working on the playroom and the extra bathroom that was added to the plans last week. So I'll have to stick around to make sure the rest of the staff stays on schedule down here."

Morgan stared at Harper for a moment before giving a little nod. "Okay, I understand. Maybe Sunday dinner next week?"

"Maybe," Harper said, and then turned to walk away.

She'd taken a couple of steps before she turned back and added, "It was nice meeting you, Garrek. Welcome home."

*Home.*

Garrek was still thinking about that word as he sat in the dining room of Gray and Morgan's house. He could refer to this place as just that because as he'd walked through, he'd noted how much the interior of the house had changed from when he lived there as a child. The living room, which was still under construction, now had larger front windows, and the floor was a darker wood than Garrek had remembered. He'd spotted a sitting room on the opposite side of the foyer, but Morgan had continued straight to the back of the house, so he'd followed her there.

They'd made a stop in the kitchen, which had a very homely feel, with the same almond-toned wood floors as the living room and sage-green cabinets. Morgan had instructed him to pick up the trays that were on the island. Garrek had been so busy looking around he'd bumped his head on one of the copper pots hanging from the large rack above the island. The sound of snickering pulled his gaze to the other side of the room, where a little boy stood with a smudge of what looked like grape jelly on his cheek.

The boy made Garrek smile, and he winked at him as he picked up the tray of bacon and the other one of sausage patties and links. He walked them into the dining room and set them on the long oak table.

Things were different in here as well. The bottom half of the walls were covered in wood that appeared to have been painted and then scraped. It was an odd look, but taking it in with the upper half of the walls, painted the color of churned butter, and the rest of the wood furniture that boasted the same distressed look, it all kind of made sense.

When he'd lived here, this room had been painted a very light brown. The table was large enough to accommodate twelve, just like this one, and heavy mustard-yellow drapes had hung from the windows. There was a large bay window where sunlight was allowed to pour into the uncovered windows, giving this space a much more cheerful look.

"Do you like biscuits and jelly?"

Garrek turned away from the window to see that the little boy had followed him.

"As a matter of fact, I do," Garrek replied and then went to grab a napkin from the table that had been neatly set for six. "But when I used to sneak some from the kitchen, I remembered to wipe the evidence from my face."

The little boy's eyes grew bigger, and he hurriedly grabbed the napkin from Garrek to wipe both of his cheeks.

Garrek smiled once more. "Good job."

"Speaking of jobs," Morgan said as she came into the dining room carrying a pitcher of orange juice in one hand and a plate stacked with French toast in the other, "why are you messing with Harper's schedule? She knows what she's doing and so far has remained on schedule." She nodded at Garrek, who had moved closer to take both the orange juice and French toast from her and set them on the table.

Gray came out of the kitchen seconds later carrying the tray of his only mildly overcooked scrambled eggs and a basket of biscuits. "But after your last doctor's appointment, I'm not so sure those two you're carrying are going to stay on schedule," he stated.

Once he sat, they were all at the table, except for the pretty little girl Garrek spied holding on to Gray's leg. Since he'd already met Jack, Garrek was sure this had to be Lily, the girl who had really captured Gray's heart. On the short ride over, his brother had been unable to talk about anything else but these twins he was now responsible for. He loved them. That had been clear to Garrek. His brother, the cool and aloof businessman, had fallen in love with two adorable children and their charming mother.

Home. Wife. Kids. The perfect storm, Garrek thought.

At one point in his life he'd thought he might want that. And then he'd thought better of the silly notion. His life was his career; that's what he'd always planned.

"Nonsense," Morgan said after she'd taken a few seconds to ease into the chair across from Gray. "I'm due September 1, and that's the perfect day for these babies to be born. It won't be in the sticky and stifling heat of the summer, but knocking on the door to fall."

She was rubbing her stomach as she spoke, and Garrek couldn't help but stare.

"I hope they're not girls," Jack said as he shifted in the seat next to Garrek.

"There's nothing wrong with girls," Gray replied while lifting Lily and placing her into the seat beside him. "They're sugar and spice and everything nice."

The kiss he planted on Lily's cheek was loud and resulted in the girl smiling as she practically beamed at him.

*Yes, they are*, Garrek thought and then shook his head to clear his mind.

"Harper works for you?" he asked Gray after the blessing had been said and everyone was busy putting food onto their plates.

"Harper owns Presley Construction. Her cousins Craig and Marlon work with the construction crew, and Harper manages the project," Gray told him.

"She's really good at what she does," Morgan added. "And she's a nice girl. So you should definitely take her out on that date you paid for."

"How much do you pay for dates?" Jack asked.

"Usually men don't pay for dates," Gray answered quickly. "But my brother wanted to make a donation to a worthy cause. Isn't that right, Garrek?"

"Ah, yeah, that's right," Garrek answered. He figured now was definitely not the right time to bring up the fact that he hadn't known he was doing any of that. He'd just been enjoying his drink. Maybe that had been a sign that he'd had enough to drink for the night.

"I think they should go to a movie and have dinner at the diner," Morgan said. "Something casual."

"I want to see *Beauty and the Beast*," Lily replied quietly.

"I don't really want to go on a date," Garrek announced.

The words had been rolling over and over in his mind

since Morgan had brought it up on the porch. He hadn't come to Temptation to date anyone. He'd had enough of that back in Washington. Garrek was here to get his thoughts together, to figure out what his next step in life was, and that did not involve Harper, the prettiest construction worker he'd ever laid eyes on.

"I mean, that's not why I came to Temptation," he corrected when he noticed Morgan and Gray's questioning gazes were on him.

"Why aren't you flying planes?" Lily asked. "Daddy says you like to fly planes all the time."

Another mistake in what was beginning to seem like a stream of them. Garrek lifted his glass and took a gulp of orange juice.

"I do like to fly planes, but I'm on leave… I mean, I'm on a vacation for a while," he corrected when he thought Lily might not understand that Garrek's commander had authorized an emergency leave chit for Garrek. So his vacation had been both impromptu and nonnegotiable. He was still pissed about that fact, but he had no intention of letting Gray or his family know about it.

"We're on vacation, too," Jack chimed in. "For the whole summer! We've got days and days to just play and sleep."

"We have to help Mama get ready for the new babies," Lily corrected her brother.

"But we can still play, too. The babies aren't coming till the fall. That's what Aunt Wendy said," Jack argued.

"Eat, both of you," Morgan stated firmly. "Granny's coming to get you at noon to go to the playground."

That was enough to silence Jack for the rest of the meal, and while Lily obeyed her mother, she continued to send questioning gazes toward Garrek. She was a pretty little girl with her black hair separated down the middle into two ponytails, the way Garrek's mother used to style his sisters' when they were young.

Olivia Taylor had loved the sextuplets she'd prayed for. Bringing the six babies—Grayson, Garrek, Gemma, Genevieve, Gage and Gia—home from the hospital thirty years ago had been the light of her life. Having a town that was just as excited about the first multiple births as they were about the revenue from the reality show the Taylor family starred in, was a joy as well. Until seven years later when it all spiraled out of control.

The constant invasion into their privacy, coupled with the scandal Theodor created by having an affair had proved to be too much for Olivia to endure. She moved her children to Pensacola. When each of them graduated, they'd all gone their separate ways, with no intention of ever returning to this small town. But look at him now.

After breakfast Gray announced that he and Garrek would clean the dishes while Morgan took Jack and Lily upstairs to get them ready for the day with their great-grandmother. Garrek had planned to spend the bulk of the day going over the papers in his room and doing more research, but he had to admit that Gray stopping by and bringing him to meet his family had been a pleasant distraction.

"You've got a great family, Gray. I'm really happy for you," Garrek said as he brought in the last of the dishes from the dining room.

Gray was at the sink scraping the remnants of the plates into the garbage disposal.

"Thanks, Garrek," he said over his shoulder. "I didn't think it was possible, but here it is."

"Yeah," Garrek said and nodded. "Life's funny that way."

He walked over to the back door and stared out the windows to a porch that was in progress and the large backyard where Garrek remembered them playing as kids.

"Life is what you decide to make of it," Gray said.

Garrek nodded. "Dad said that at our graduation."

"He did."

"I didn't think you were listening to him. You never made it a secret that you hated him," Garrek replied without turning to look at his brother.

"I didn't hate him," Gray answered. "I hated what he did to us."

"The affair or leaving?" Garrek asked, because their father had done both. He'd had an affair with one of the production assistants from the *Taylors of Temptation* reality show, which their entire family had starred in from the time Garrek was born until he was seven years old.

"It doesn't matter," Gray said. "He's gone. Mom's gone. All of that happened a long time ago."

Garrek agreed with that, but still, he couldn't help but wonder if some mistakes were hereditary.

"I opened a new account and transferred the money under my name," Garrek told Gray. "If my commanders found out I had an offshore account, it could be a problem."

That had been his reason for taking the money that his father had apparently saved for him. Theodor Taylor had left his wife and six children for a younger woman, but he'd never stopped taking care of his family. That was obvious by the child support payments their mother always received on time, the gifts their father routinely provided for them as they were growing up and the money he'd put into accounts on Grand Cayman Island for each of his children. Money that Garrek had no idea what he was going to do with.

"It's yours to do with as you please," Gray said. "That's why I sent everyone the account information."

Gray had sent that information, along with a sealed envelope that Garrek had just opened two days ago.

"How long are you planning to stay?" Gray asked him.

Garrek turned to see his brother loading the dishwasher. He moved to the counter and picked up a damp white cloth. Without another thought, he went to the island and began to wipe it clean.

"I don't know," he answered finally. "This wasn't a planned trip, but I've got a lot of thinking to do about that stuff you sent me, so I'm going to take my time with that."

"Is that okay with your commander?" Gray asked. "Gen and I have been talking about how hard you work and how you're rising in the ranks. You sure you can be away now?"

Garrek paused and lifted his head to look at Gray, who was now standing on the other side of the island.

"Yeah, it's cool. I just want to take care of a few things before accepting my next post."

Gray stared at him for a few seconds before nodding. "Well, like I said, you're welcome to stay here."

When Garrek opened his mouth to reply, Gray held up both hands.

"But it's cool if you don't. I understand. It wasn't easy for me when I first came back here, either. I do, however, want you to come over for Sunday dinners and to spend time with us. We're family, Garrek. I know we haven't acted like it in the last ten years, but I think it's past time we started living up to what Mom always wanted."

Olivia had been proud of Garrek when he'd decided to enroll in the Naval Academy. She'd visited him in Annapolis and beamed at him in his dress uniform. Garrek could still hear the last words she'd spoken to him that day at the airport.

*You're going to be a fine pilot and an extraordinary man, Garrek. I know it here in my heart.*

The memory almost brought tears to his eyes as Garrek thought about the past few weeks and how the choices he'd made would have been such a letdown to his mother.

"Ah, I will," Garrek said and cleared his throat. "I'm going to head back to the B&B now. I'll catch up with you later."

He moved quickly, afraid that if he had to stand in that charming kitchen staring at his brother, now a father and a husband, a moment longer, he would crack. He did not want to break down, and least of all in front of Gray. So Garrek moved quickly out of the house, so fast that he almost stepped off the curb before spotting the tractor-trailer speeding down the street.

He did, however, look up in enough time to see that Harper was carrying two huge bags of something over her shoulder in a way that blocked her view of the tractor-trailer and its fast trek toward her. Garrek ran into the street and pushed Harper out of the way. They landed on the other side of the street, the bags going one way, Harper flat on her back and Garrek on top of her.

Time seemed to stand still. Everything and everyone around them also disappeared. Or rather, Garrek tuned it all out as he looked down at her. Yes, her body was soft and his was definitely responding quickly to the new physical arrangement. But it was her eyes that reached out and grabbed him, holding every part of his body completely still. It was fear, stark and bold in the depths of her eyes. He couldn't look away. Not from the orbs that resembled drops of root beer.

"I'm okay now," she said in a breathy whisper.

She pushed at him, her palms moving between them to flatten on his chest. The blood that had been pooling in his groin heated, and his erection pressed painfully against the zipper of his jeans.

"Garrek," she started once more.

He liked the sound of his name on her lips and dragged his gaze from her eyes to watch her lips move. Bare lips that were shaped like those of the heavily made-up women he saw in magazine ads. Her nose was long, straight and peppered with freckles. It wasn't a usual feature he saw on women, but damn, on her it was more than a little arousing.

"What happened?" a male voice asked.

"Are you all right, Harper?" came another.

It was then that Garrek realized a few things. One, they were not alone, and two, he was still on top of her. And he was enjoying being on top of her, much more than he ever would have anticipated.

"I'm okay," she said and pushed at him hard enough this time that he moved.

As he came to stand, Garrek took her by both hands and helped her up. When she was standing, she immediately pulled her hands from his grip.

"What the hell was that?" A tall guy dressed in cargo pants and a T-shirt came over to move between Garrek and Harper. "Are you all right?"

"I'm good," Harper told him, but he didn't seem convinced. "Really, Marlon, I'm okay."

Garrek looked at the guy differently now. At first he'd been wondering if it were her boyfriend or something like that. But he remembered hearing her say the name before, and Morgan saying that Marlon and Craig were her cousins who worked for her. So he relaxed a little when he replied, "A tractor-trailer going way too fast in this residential area."

Marlon turned to stare at him. He was a young guy, maybe midtwenties, with a bush of curly dark hair and a beard.

"And you are?" Marlon asked.

Garrek extended his hand and answered, "I'm Garrek Taylor."

It wasn't until he said *Taylor* that Marlon's stance eased and he shook Garrek's hand. Garrek could totally understand protective cousins.

"We need to get back to work," Harper said, and the others who had gathered around them began to scatter.

Garrek didn't move, and neither did Marlon.

"Thanks, Garrek," she said as she looked over to him. "I should have been paying more attention."

After that Harper walked away with Marlon following her. Garrek figured the guy still wasn't a hundred percent certain about him. Perhaps because of the way he'd been lying comfortably—or at least pleasurably— on top of Harper. But Garrek wasn't concerned with Marlon or his perception of him at the moment. He was mesmerized, once again, by the way Harper's jeans fit her and how her long legs carried her gracefully across the street. When she squatted to pick up one of the bags she'd been carrying, Garrek continued to watch her, noting the strength in her arms and the independence in her spirit as she refused Marlon's help.

He stared at her for much longer than was probably proper, and when he finally decided to turn away and started walking down the street, he was still thinking of her. With everything else he had going on in his life, the very last thing he needed was to have another woman on his mind. But she was there, her face apparently permanently etched in his mind, the feel of her beneath him emblazoned on his body. Even the air he breathed seemed to smell just like her—an earthy, floral mixture that was driving him crazy.

When he finally arrived at the B&B Garrek went straight to his room and dropped down into a chair. He ran his hands over his face and shook his head in an attempt to erase the current thoughts. Harper Presley was not what Garrek needed to be thinking about right now. He already had one woman wreaking havoc in his life. He definitely did not need another one.

## Chapter 4

He was hard.

Strong…she meant.

And hard.

And the memory of him stuck in her mind like rocks in cement.

It had been about seven hours since Garrek Taylor had saved her life—from the idiot tractor-trailer driver who had been illegally speeding down a residential street. Almost twenty-four hours since he'd saved her from the Magnolia Guild and further humiliation in front of a small portion of the town's population. And a little less than that since he'd invaded her dreams with his sexy voice and that knowing glare.

Truth be told, Harper wasn't overly worried about what the townspeople thought about her. They'd been thinking the same thing all her life—that Harper Lane Presley was an incorrigible tomboy who'd rather swallow flies than wear a dress and makeup. They were partially right. Harper did not like makeup. She'd tried it once and her stubborn freckles had poked right through, like tenacious weeds growing in a garden year after year. And dresses did not work well with climbing trees or playing softball and sliding into home to score the winning run, which was the ultimate act to show off in front of her cousins.

But she was not incorrigible. In fact, when Harper had left Temptation to attend Virginia Varsity University, where she'd studied building construction, she'd actually made a concerted effort to try to act like the other girls. That hadn't ended well, and Harper decided then that she simply was who she was, and whoever had a problem with that just didn't matter.

Garrek Taylor didn't seem to have a problem with her. He'd shown that with his twenty-five-hundred-dollar bid. Did that make him an ass? Bidding on a woman like she was a piece of property instead of doing the sociable thing and asking for a date like an ordinary man? Or did that mean he'd liked what he'd seen as she stood on that stage in one of the few skirts she owned, praying for a way to escape? She didn't know, and she shouldn't even be worrying about it. She couldn't go on a date with Garrek Taylor.

She did, however, if she were totally truthful with herself, want to feel his hard body against hers once more. Sure, he had done it to save her life, but Harper had immediately realized that there were worse scenarios than having a man who looked—and oh, yes, smelled—like Garrek lying on top of her. His cologne was a bold musk fragrance that screamed strength and confidence even louder than his stance and actions.

She'd picked up his scent last night as he'd walked beside her. Had dreamed about it last night and almost swooned over it when he'd been standing right behind her on the porch this morning. By the time he was on top of her, she'd been ready to rip his clothes off and press them to her nose. Damn, she was pitiful.

"There you are. I've been looking for you. We've got company."

Harper startled at the sound of her father's voice. She'd been standing at the railing on the back porch of her family farm, staring out at the miles of grass that led down to the barn.

"Oh, Daddy, I'm not in the mood for guests—" Her words were lost as Harper moved away from the railing and turned to see the company her father was referring to.

"Garrek here says you two met last night. Then Craig and Marlon told me about the incident at the Taylor house this afternoon. Why didn't you tell me?"

Arnold Presley was a retired marine colonel. He was six feet three inches tall and almost as wide as a doorway. He kept his bulky frame in good physical condition by doing all the lifting and hauling around the farm. And according to him, he exercised his brain by watching an even mix of CNN and *Sanford and Son* reruns. His gray hair was cut close, while his keen sense for people ran rampant all day long.

"Last night was ridiculous and not worth talking about. Except that Mr., ah… Garrek Taylor…he um, made a great contribution to the Veterans Fund. So that was the highlight," she said, managing to keep her gaze from falling on Garrek, who stood just behind her father.

He'd changed clothes. Earlier he'd worn jeans and a

T-shirt. Tonight, he had on blue slacks and a gray button-down shirt. From laid-back to business casual, he
looked like a model. Everything fit just the right way,
and he appeared perfect in everything. It would have
been sickening—if it wasn't so alluring.

"Well, I would expect nothing less of a military man,"
Arnold continued.

He was smiling—which her father rarely did—when
he reached over to slap his brawny hand on Garrek's
shoulder. If that action caused Garrek any pain or dis-
comfort, he was an expert at not showing his emotions,
because he only smiled at Arnold and then returned his
inquisitive gaze to her.

"You're in the service?" she asked.

"Navy," he replied.

"He's a navy pilot!" Arnold added. "I'll excuse him
for choosing the navy over the FRS."

Arnold thought everybody who even considered a
career in the military should select the marines. How
many debates had she witnessed between her father and
her grandfather about which was better, the marines or
the army? Too many to count.

"I didn't know that," she said, folding her arms across
her chest. "Well, I'm sure my father will keep you enter-
tained with talk about the war or the service, or both. I've
got a few things to check, so I'll just get out of your way."

She made it all the way into the living room before
she was stopped.

"Never seen you run from anybody before."

"What?" she asked and spun around to see her grandfather sitting in his favorite recliner.

Harper hated that chair. The dingy brown floral pat-
tern was straight out of the '60s, and it creaked every

time Pops leaned back to recline in it. But two Christ-
mases ago when she'd bought him a new motorized
leather recliner, he'd thanked her kindly but flat out refused to sit in it, declaring there was nothing wrong with
his old one. The new recliner made its way into her father's bedroom, and Harper wisely never broached the
subject of Pops's favorite seat in the house again.

"Oh, Pops, you scared me," she replied.

"Only reason somebody would be frightened in
their own house is if they were doing something they
shouldn't be doing," he quipped.

He was sitting back in that chair, legs crossed at the
ankles and pouring tobacco into his pipe, while his wire-
framed glasses slipped slightly down his nose.

"Who's frightened? I'm heading to the barn to make
sure Craig stacked all the boxes of tile along the side like
I asked him to. Aunt Laura called him and Marlon home
right after we finished up today, so he said he'd bring
the tile by after the special dinner she had planned."

Pops nodded and took the first puff of his pipe. He'd
been lighting it while she talked. That's how she'd known
she'd been rambling, because he hadn't looked up once.

"Laura celebrates everything. I think Giff said it was
the anniversary of the day they moved into that house.
That's why she was having a big ol' dinner. Your father
told Giff we already had our dinner on the stove when
he called. That way we wouldn't have to go."

Harper frowned. "We had smoked sausage and fried
potatoes for dinner tonight, and Daddy didn't start cooking that until after I was home and showered."

"Yep," Pops said and gave his wide, toothy smile.
"You're right about that."

Harper smiled in return, because her grandfather's

bug eyes, those glasses and his grin always made her feel happy inside.

"Right. So I'm just going to go out and get a count. I might load them in my truck so I'll be ready to leave early tomorrow."

"Sure. Sure. Take all the time you need," Pops said. "I'm sure that nice navy fella will be gone by the time you're done."

Harper knew exactly what he was trying to say. But he was wrong anyway—she wasn't running from Garrek Taylor. There was no reason to run from a man who meant nothing to her, but who still managed to set every inch of her traitorous body on fire with one gaze.

"He didn't come to see me, Pops. So it's fine if I leave," she said and moved closer to the door.

"Guess you're right. He came all the way out here to meet two old duds like me and your dad."

Harper kept going, muttering once more, "He didn't come to see me," before opening and closing the front door behind her.

Garrek had driven out to the Presley farm to make sure that Harper was all right. After the near accident this morning, he'd just wanted to make sure he hadn't hurt her with his impromptu save-the-day act. She was a lot thinner than his two hundred and thirty pounds.

He also wanted to get his mind off the many papers he'd read while he enjoyed the room service meal earlier this evening. A stout woman with tightly curled, frosted gray hair had welcomed him back when he arrived at the B&B after leaving Gray's house. She'd introduced herself as Mrs. Louisa Reed, but insisted Garrek call her Nana Lou and apologized profusely for any bad things he might have heard about her son, Harry—who was now in jail—and Gray's wife. Nana Lou felt the need to cater to him personally, even though there was another man at the front desk when he'd come in. His name was Otis, and the old herringbone cap he wore had definitely seen better days.

Garrek had found the scene to be homely and welcoming, a stark contrast from life on the base, or flying out at a moment's notice for secret flight exercises. It made him think once more about the life he'd chosen, the one he'd thought he wanted more than anything else.

A few hours later, Nana Lou had sent up a large bowl of beef stew with two thick chunks of warm homemade bread and a pitcher of lemonade. It was a humid June day, and yet the hearty stew and bread had hit the spot as an early dinner in the quaint air-conditioned room. While he enjoyed the stew, Garrek read through everything in the two envelopes that Gray had sent him months ago. After the meal, he sat in the high-backed chair near the window and thought about everything that had been in those envelopes. When he finally felt a bit overwhelmed with it all, the idea to check on Harper hit him. And Otis had been the one to provide her address when Garrek inquired.

He'd hoped the ride would clear his mind, but it only gave him more time to contemplate what was happening in his life. First: a house.

In addition to the three million dollars, Theodor Taylor had also left something called the Adberry house to his second son. After receiving Gray's packages six months ago, Garrek had decided to deal with the money first. Once the new accounts were open, he'd also put copies of the paperwork from all the accounts, and the letter from Gray detailing how he'd found the money their father had left to each of them, in a safe-deposit box. Garrek had never been stationed out of the country so there was no reason for him to have an account in Grand Cayman. Sure, it was an inheritance and having an offshore account didn't necessarily equate to wrongdoing, but after being linked to a family with one national scandal in his lifetime Garrek had no desire to tempt fate. He'd never had a blemish on his record with the military and he didn't want to take the chance of his commanding officers finding out and getting the wrong idea.

That had been easy enough to deal with. As for this house, he wasn't quite sure about that one yet, especially since he'd been on the fence about Gray selling their father's other properties in Temptation.

So by the time Garrek had arrived at the farm, he was more than ready to see Harper's pretty face again. There was something about her that he had yet to figure out that made him want—no, need—to see her. It was the oddest thing. He had come to Temptation to get away from one woman, only to have another one plague his thoughts. And this one, unlike the woman he'd left in Washington, didn't want his attention at all.

Linus and Arnold Presley were nice enough men who were more than eager to talk about their respective military careers. But since Garrek wasn't sure he was going to have a military career in the upcoming weeks, he didn't welcome the topic of conversation. The only other thing that captivated the men's attention was when he said, "I came to make sure Harper was all right."

They'd each perked up at that comment, which had surprised Garrek.

"Oh, yeah, she seemed fine at dinner," Arnold said. "My nephew Marlon called to tell us about the incident."

"And I immediately called Sherriff Duncan and told him to get his butt in gear. Tractor-trailers aren't supposed to be on residential streets. Highways and main thoroughfares is what the town ordinance says," Linus added.

"Well, I'm just glad it turned out the way it did," Garrek replied. "She seems to have vanished, though, before I could really talk to her."

"Oh, no, I know just where you can find her," Linus announced as he puffed on his pipe.

That's how Garrek ended up walking about fifteen feet from the main house and around the side of a huge barn. It was already getting dark, but he moved about, ignoring the sound of whichever animals were kept on this farm. He found her when he rounded the last corner that would have taken him into a complete circle. She was loading the back of a pickup truck with heavy-looking boxes, bending over so that he once again had an unfettered view of her shapely bottom.

"Here, let me do that," he said, coming up behind her and attempting to take the box she'd just lifted.

"What? Oh, no. I have it." She held on to the box.

He pulled on his end. "I said I'll do it for you. These are heavy."

She huffed and gave another tug. "I can handle it. It's my job, and I don't need any help."

Garrek did not move, but held her irritated gaze. "There's no need for us to argue. I'm just trying to be nice."

"I don't need you to be nice to me. I'm perfectly capable of moving out of the way when a truck speeds toward me. And I've been lifting heavy boxes on construction sites since I was ten years old," she said and tugged on the box once more. "And furthermore, I'm also perfectly capable of getting my own date! Thank you very much!"

At those last words, Garrek let go of the box. Apparently she wasn't holding on as tightly as he'd thought, because his actions forced her back a step until she hit the edge of the open truck bed. The box slipped from her hands and fell to the ground with a thump.

"What did you just say?" he asked.

She was slightly winded, her chest moving up and down quickly, strands of hair that had been pulled back when he approached now touching the sides of her face.

"I…I, um, I said I don't need your help with the boxes," she told him.

Garrek took a step closer to her. He should have been moving in the other direction. In fact, he shouldn't have come out here in the first place. It was apparent that she was just fine. She'd looked more than fine when she'd walked away from him earlier today. She'd looked stubborn, independent and beautiful.

"No, the other thing you said," he stated, his voice going lower.

She licked her lips, and Garrek bit back a moan.

"I already thanked you for saving my life," she said. "You didn't have to come all the way out here. Isn't that like stalking?"

He was closer now, so close that she tried to back up but ended up sitting on the edge of the truck bed. He moved quickly then, because if he gave himself one moment to think about what he was doing, he would turn and run as far as he could get from this farm. This was crazy and ridiculous. It was reckless and stupid in light of all he'd been through in the past few months. At the same time, Garrek knew that nothing short of lightning striking at that truck was going to stop what was about to happen.

"You said something else," he whispered. "About getting a date for yourself."

"I can," she insisted and tried to scoot back farther onto the truck.

Boxes already stacked in the truck bed hindered her progress, and Garrek pushed her knees apart to stand between them. He wrapped his arms around her waist and pulled so that she slid snugly up against him. Her hands slapped against his chest and she pushed at him. It was a light, unconvincing push; otherwise he would have been forced to back away.

"I didn't need you to pay to go out with me," she said.

"I didn't," he replied. "At least I didn't know that was what was going on at the time."

Her eyes grew wide then, and for a moment Garrek wasn't sure if it was because of what he'd said or the fact that his hands had slid beneath her bottom, cupping her gently.

"They were taking bids on dates for me," she said with a tinge of hurt.

"They were being idiots," he said and lowered his face to hers.

She shook her head then. "If you weren't bidding on me, why did you pay the money?"

That was the million-dollar question. And up until this moment he hadn't admitted the answer, not even to himself.

"Because the moment I realized what was happening I wanted to fix it for you. Had I simply walked off that stage, I figured you would have been further humiliated.

I was trying to make things better for you," he stated, the words leaving a warmth in his chest that he wasn't totally sure wasn't the beginning of a coronary event.

"You don't even know me," she said, and dammit, she licked her lips again.

It was as if she couldn't help it. Just like he couldn't help what he was about to do next.

He moved in closer, until the tip of his nose brushed against the tip of hers.

"What are you doing?" she asked, her voice just the barest whisper of warmth across his face.

Garrek tilted his head. "Getting this out of the way," he said, and then touched his lips to hers.

It sounded like a simple act, though it was anything but. Her lips were warm against his, and when his tongue slid alongside hers, there was an explosion in his mind, behind the closed lids of his eyes and spreading throughout every recess of his body. It seemed as if the earth moved, or something equally jolting, but Garrek did not let her go. He couldn't.

What he did was pull her even closer, letting his hands move down the backs of her legs until he had them fastened behind his back. Her hands were still on his chest, but her fingers had clenched in his shirt as she leaned into the kiss. Her mouth was hungry, her teeth nipping against his lips when he pulled away slightly. So Garrek sank deep once more, tasting her the way he would have a delectable dessert.

She was wrapped tightly around him and he felt her bottom once more, squeezing her mounds in his hands and this time letting that moan break free. This was it—this right here was what he'd really come out to this farm for. This one unforgettable kiss.

# Chapter 5

His lips felt every bit as good as she'd imagined they would. That thought had come to Harper just as her tongue moved languidly against his for what felt like the billionth time. She was drifting, floating on a fluffy cloud of pleasure. At least that's what this kiss felt like.

He held her so tightly against him, his mouth moving masterfully over hers. Harper sighed into the kiss, letting her hands move upward to cup the back of his head and hold him to her. He'd wrapped her legs around him just as she had imagined it.

Last night she'd imagined all sorts of things about Garrek Taylor. But she would have never conjured the way he had so dominantly taken her on the bed of her truck. Now she knew that it would be emblazoned in her memory forever.

She was drowning. Harper was sure of it. Drowning

in the delicious taste of him as surely as he was feasting on her. His moans told the story. He was enjoying this kiss just as much as she was. She didn't know what to think of that.

Correction, she *couldn't* think. Not right now. Because if she did…

The memory was quick and ferocious, flashing through her mind like a lightning bolt. On her next inhale, the pain spread through her chest so that she was immediately turning her head away from Garrek, effectively severing the connection of their lips. She gasped and tried to take in as much oxygen as she could. The effort only caused more pain, until she was heaving and panting so loudly that he moved back. His hands were on her arms now, shaking her gently until she looked up at him.

"Harper? Are you all right?"

He was speaking. She could hear him, but her vision had gone blurry and her body began to shake. She wasn't all right. After all this time, she still wasn't all right.

"I have to go," Harper finally managed to say.

She pushed at his arms and eased off the truck when he dropped his hands from her and took a step back.

"Harper," he said. "I'm sorry."

She was already walking away from him when she heard the words. There'd never been an apology before. She would have liked one, but it never came.

"Good night, Garrek," she said and walked as fast as she could—refusing to run again—until she was at the house.

There, she took the front steps two at a time and quickly crossed the wood-plank porch until she reached the screen door. Inside, she ran. Straight upstairs to the room that had belonged to her since she was five years old. Once there, Harper closed the door and fell back against it. She stuffed her fist into her mouth to stifle the cry of pain and sorrow, and, yes, of regret. Because no matter how hard she tried, no matter how hard she worked, Harper knew she would never get over her past. And as long as she couldn't get over her past, dreaming about doing more with a man like Garrek was not a possibility.

A week had passed since Harper had spoken to Garrek. She'd seen him, because she worked at his brother's house five days a week and because Temptation was a very small town. Especially when there was someone to be avoided.

She should be used to it by now—the flaming feeling surfacing in her cheeks and the sweaty palms. She was a mess and was smart enough to admit that, at least to herself. But she didn't have to show it.

All week long, Harper had gone to work and focused solely on her job. From the time she was thirteen years old and spent the day at her uncle Giff's lumberyard, she knew she'd found her refuge. She gained a feeling of accomplishment from building something new. Planning how it would look and then working with her hands to see that it came to fruition.

It was that summer when she'd followed her uncle from one end of the lumberyard to the other, riding with him as he delivered pieces of furniture he made, or shipments of lumber that went to construction sites in neighboring towns, that she'd decided what her future would be. At that moment, she'd committed herself to learning everything about the construction business so that one day she could build on her own. New homes, renovations, upgrades—all of it had been her goal. And finally, that day had come.

The Taylor house was the biggest project for her two-year-old company to date. And Harper knew that having this job turn out well and gaining a recommendation from Gray Taylor was going to put her into the big league. With Gray's connections around the world, she was sure to pick up more jobs in the Virginia area, and for Harper, that meant everything. Even Morgan's word carried weight in this town. Most of the women had already adored Morgan as she taught their children at the elementary school. As for the men, they'd come to rally behind Morgan some months back when she and Gray had uncovered the connection between Harry Reed and Gray's former assistant, Kym Hutchins. Those two had been arrested for burning down the community center.

Harper had always liked Morgan's friendly nature. She enjoyed Morgan's sister, Wendy, as well, and had often sat with the ladies at town meetings and church functions because nobody seemed to bother them. That was most likely because Ida Mae Bonet was known for protecting her granddaughters like a regal mother hen. Harper loved Ms. Ida, especially since she'd grown up without the benefit of her own mother or grandmother.

Jaclyn Presley had died from complications of pneumonia when Harper was just four years old. And since her father was stationed overseas at the time, Harper had been taken in by her uncle Giff and aunt Laura, who were still living in the farmhouse her grandparents had bought thirty years before. When her aunt and uncle finally found their own home, Harper hadn't wanted to leave the farm, and rather than cause her any more distress, Linus Presley had announced that she would live right there with him.

Harper had grown to love that big rambling house that

sat on sixty-four acres of land. She'd also enjoyed being out at the farm, away from all the whispers and stares of the townspeople. That was when she was young; now that she was an adult, Harper recognized the need to hold her head up high and conduct herself with the highest level of professionalism and integrity, even if most of the time she felt like slapping every one of the busybodies who commented on her single status and so-called boyish appearance.

"Mama says we have to be careful not to get the white dirty," a small girl's voice spoke.

It was a pleasant sound that effectively interrupted Harper's thoughts.

"Oh, but I used a washable paint, so things like fingerprints and smudges can be easily wiped off," Harper told Lily, who had quietly come out onto the back porch where she was working today.

Morgan wanted an enclosed porch that would provide an outdoor space her family could enjoy no matter the weather. So Harper followed the original slanted roofline, repairing all the existing shingles and then adding new, more supportive beams to the entire structure. French doors led down the double-wide stairs into the backyard. The furniture—a complete living room set and six-foot table with benches—would be delivered tomorrow. Royal blue and yellow would be the accent colors out here.

"Jack's messy when he paints," Lily added as she held her doll close.

The little girl wore pale green shorts and a white shirt with green-and-yellow polka dots. She was only five years old but had a mature way about her that reminded Harper of herself when she was younger. Only for Harper, there had been no playing with dolls or dressing up. She'd had nobody to do that with, since her cousins were boys.

"It'll be fine," Harper told her. "I'm sure you'll teach him how to be neat."

Lily nodded and walked to the other end of the porch. She was adorable, her little hands lightly touching the knob on one of the French doors. Harper had just finished inspecting the floors. They'd decided on wooden planks with a worn look that would continue the rustic-chic decor that Morgan had implemented throughout the house. Because they were on a tight schedule, yesterday's installation had been done during hours of thunderstorms and humidity. Today, Harper wanted to make sure there was no buckling.

"Boys are hard to teach," Lily announced.

Harper couldn't help but smile at the comment. "You might be right about that."

"Oh, I don't know. I think I learn pretty quickly."

Harper spun around so fast at that voice, she stumbled back against the corner wall where she'd been standing.

"Uncle Garrek!" Lily exclaimed before running across the floor to jump up into his arms.

He lifted her high above his head, and she giggled. Harper righted herself and swallowed. She had to get herself together, or Garrek Taylor was sure to think she was as flighty as they came in this town.

"Ready for our picnic?" Garrek asked Lily when he'd settled her on his hip.

Harper tried to go on with her work, moving to another corner and then pulling out her tape measure to be sure the table that Morgan had insisted on was going to fit on this side of the porch.

"Yup. I'm ready," Lily replied.

Harper was leaning over slightly to read the measurements on the tape when she suddenly felt warm.

"Are you ready, Harper?" he asked about two seconds before she quickly stood upright and found her backside flush against his front.

"Whoa," Garrek said with a chuckle as his arm wrapped easily around her waist, holding her to him. "Be careful. Wouldn't want you to hurt yourself."

He'd whispered those last words in her ear, and Harper had immediately moved out of his reach as the warmth traveled quickly down her side. Where was Lily? Hadn't Garrek just been holding her in his arms? If so, how could he now be standing so close…too close to her?

Harper spotted Lily standing a few feet away from them and quickly cleared her throat before speaking, "Ah, I'm…um, yes, I'm ready to finish up my work here. I also have to check in on the progress of the playroom and…"

"You gotta eat like the rest of the staff," Lily stated. "That's what Uncle Garrek said."

Harper looked to Garrek, who had glanced from his niece and back to Harper with a sheepish grin.

"We'll fix a nice lunch and take it down to the lake," he said.

"She won't say no because she usually eats when the rest of the staff does." The child even attempted to mimic her uncle's voice as she spoke.

Harper might have smiled at that if Lily's diatribe didn't give away Garrek's duplicity.

"Did I get it right, Uncle Garrek?" Lily finished, looking up at Garrek earnestly when the silence stretched on.

Garrek chuckled and then nodded to his niece. "You got it just right, pretty girl."

"I don't understand," Harper said, even though she thought she was close to figuring it out.

Garrek was going to ask her to lunch. The question now was, would she go?

"We want you to come have lunch with us," Lily announced.

If Harper wasn't feeling so uneasy, she might have been amused by the slightly exasperated look Lily was now giving her.

"Oh, no, I have too much work to do, Lily. But it's a lovely day, so you two should go ahead and enjoy yourselves," Harper told her quickly.

What was he trying to do? Was this his way of getting the date he'd paid for?

"All work and no play makes Harper—" Garrek started before being interrupted by Jack, who came running out onto the porch with a baseball bat in one hand, a ball in the other.

"I'm ready, Uncle Garrek! Had to get my baseball stuff. My dad says I'm getting good at hitting," Jack told Garrek as he looked up at him with admiration.

Lily shook her head, as if Jack's words made no sense at all. "Dads are supposed to say nice things to their children," she told him.

The look Jack shot her over his shoulder was filled with just enough annoyance that Harper finally grinned. She could easily recall how often she'd solicited that very look from Craig and Marlon when they were younger.

"Shall we get going before another world war starts?" Garrek asked her.

He was also grinning, probably remembering his interactions with his siblings when they were younger as well. That thought had Harper wondering what type of child Garrek had been. As an adult, he struck her as being serious and self-assured. Today, he was also devilishly handsome in his khaki shorts and Orioles baseball jersey. But that definitely wasn't something Harper should be thinking about.

"I'm really busy," she began, but he was already shaking his head.

"It's just lunch, Harper. And the children will be with us, so you have nothing to worry about."

As if she was worried about being alone with him.

Except that she was. Kinda.

"Fine," she finally replied with a huff. "Picnic lunch it is. But we're taking my truck down to the lake."

She wanted at least that much control over this situation that had seemed to sneak up on her.

Garrek didn't remember the lake.

In the last week, he realized there was a lot about Temptation that he hadn't remembered. This town had once been his home, but now it seemed like a totally different place. One he'd never imagined himself in again. Yet here he was. He hadn't thought too much about why in the last few days, but had focused instead on the current matters at hand. He had a house and an inheritance. A niece and nephew, and two more on the way. His brother, whom he hadn't spent time with in years, and a sister-in-law who was just as spirited and remarkable as his sisters.

He also had a woman whom he hadn't been able to stop thinking about, no matter how hard he tried. At this moment, that woman was instructing Jack on how to properly swing a bat.

"Ready for the first pitch?" Garrek asked from about ten feet away.

Jack had on his helmet and was standing with his small legs spread, his elbows slightly lifted as he did exactly what Harper told him. To Garrek's right, still sitting on the blanket where they'd had their lunch twenty minutes ago, Lily sat playing with the doll she'd brought along. The doll—Susie—was being stubborn and wouldn't finish her carrots. "Children need their vegetables," Lily said patiently to Susie.

"They sure do," Harper said before picking up one of the baby carrots from the plastic bowl and popping it into her mouth.

This made Lily smile and take a carrot herself. She put it into her mouth and chewed while looking at Harper and nodding.

"Ready!" Harper yelled to him and, thankful for the blast of reality, Garrek readied himself to toss the ball.

Jack looked serious, biting on his lower lip as he made eye contact with Garrek. He was concentrating, just like Harper had told him. Watching the pitcher, preparing himself for when the ball left Garrek's hand. Knowing all this, Garrek wanted another couple of seconds before tossing the ball. Not too fast and not too slow, straight toward his nephew's bat. Jack took the swing and tapped the ball so that it soared a whopping two feet in front of him. He dropped the bat at that point and jumped up and down, his cheers of joy causing an infectious reaction as Garrek lifted his own arms in victory as well. Harper clapped and leaned down with her hand up to meet Jack's for a high five.

"I did it! I did it!" Jack was yelling when Garrek came to stand close to him. "I hit the ball, Uncle Garrek! Ms. Harper showed me how!"

"You sure did, buddy," Garrek said as he too gave Jack a high five. "Good job!"

"I get to have cookies now," Jack exclaimed and immediately took off to join his sister on the blanket, where he grabbed the plastic bowl filled with cookies.

Harper was smiling when Garrek turned from Jack to her. The gentle breeze lifted the edges of her hair, rays from the sun causing her brown eyes to look a bit lighter today.

"You like to play sports?" he asked.

It wasn't the smoothest or most logical question to ask, but for whatever reason, she always managed to make him forget the way he usually acted around women.

She shrugged and lifted a hand to tuck the flyaway strands of hair behind her ear. "I grew up with my grandfather, uncle and two male cousins. I had to like sports."

Garrek knew that Harper's mother had died when she was young and that her grandfather, uncle and aunt had raised her. He also knew that the town considered her a hopeless tomboy who would eventually turn into an old spinster, hence the reason the Magnolia Guild had attempted to find her a date.

"I liked planes," he replied.

"That's why you became a pilot?"

She remembered what he did for a living. Garrek would take that as a point in his favor, considering she was the first woman to ever hyperventilate and then run away from his kiss.

"It's all I ever wanted to do," he said.

"Like I wanted to build things. It's good to have a dream and be able to realize it," she said and stuffed her hands into the front pockets of her jeans.

He'd never known a woman could look so sexy and

enticing in something as simple as worn jeans and a T-shirt. But Harper did. Each day he'd watched her work or simply walk from the house to her truck, climb up on a ladder or stand with clipboard in hand instructing her staff. She always looked good. That fact no longer amazed him; it aroused him. Every time.

"Dreams are what life is made of," he said. "My mother used to tell us that."

"Your mother was a very smart and dear woman. That's what I heard. I didn't know her, but my aunt Laura did."

Garrek nodded. He'd been bumping into a lot of people in town who had known his mother and the rest of their family. They knew about his father's rumored affair and the demise of the Taylor family's reality show. What they didn't seem to know was that the Taylor sextuplets had thrived after they were no longer on television. Despite all that they'd been through, they'd made it past the turmoil and were now happy, healthy, successful adults. At least that's what Garrek had been telling himself all these years.

"She was a great mother and an even better friend," he replied.

Harper nodded. "You miss her."

"I do," he admitted.

"Is that why you came back to Temptation?"

"No" was his quick reply.

She tilted her head to stare at him, her questioning look clear. She wanted to know why, but she wouldn't push. He liked that. He liked her. Much more than he should.

"I came back to claim the house my father left to me. I'd like your help in doing that," he said, once again surprising himself—and from the look on Harper's face, her, too.

## Chapter 6

Adberry House was breathtaking.

Harper stood at the bottom of the front steps and looked up at the sprawling structure in awe.

"Joffrey Adberry fought in the Civil War. He left his family—Ester, his wife, Margaret and Ellen, his daughters, and Sarabelle, his mother-in-law—here in this house. They owned twenty-two slaves, fifteen horses and a hundred-acre tobacco field," she said, knowing the story of this antebellum home as if it were her own personal history.

"My father bought this house two months before my mother died. They'd been divorced for fifteen years by that time. In a letter to her, he wrote about how she'd always loved this place and the dream of seeing all her children running around this land instead of working on it. She wanted a garden and tall trees and to have parties for the people of the town to share this piece of history with them. He planned to give it to her. But he was too late."

Garrek sounded distant as he spoke, even though he was standing only two feet away from her. It had taken three days for them to arrange a time that was suitable for them both to meet here. She wasn't sure what other business Garrek had in town, but she knew her schedule had quickly turned hectic when, as she'd feared, the wood floors on the back porch buckled after two days of rainstorms, so the entire porch had to be redone. In addition, while renovating one of the upstairs bedrooms, they'd come across a leak that required major roof repairs. She was exhausted, and it was almost nine o'clock in the evening. But she'd agreed to this time because Garrek had gone to dinner with Gray, Morgan and Mr. Simon from the historical society.

When Marlon had gone for coffee and doughnuts this morning, he'd overheard Millie talking to Clarice about seeing the Taylors at dinner. Clarice Conyers owned the Java Shop. She was also Connie from the Magnolia Guild's younger sister. Marlon had delivered the details of this conversation directly to Harper, even though she wasn't totally sure why.

"My father says a man who loved his wife completely would give her the moon and the stars if he could. Your father giving your mother this house says a lot about his feelings for her," she told Garrek. She hoped it made him feel better than he sounded at the moment, but his expression didn't change.

"He cheated on her and then walked away from all of us. That said a lot about his feelings, too" was Garrek's cool reply. "Let's get inside before it rains again."

This was said just as curtly, but Harper dismissed that because while he'd spoken, he'd also grabbed her hand in his and led them up the old steps.

They didn't creak eerily, but the boards were loose and in obvious need of repair. The numerous columns that stretched for at least eight feet from the floor of the porch to the first landing still seemed sturdy but were definitely in need of a paint job. Night had just settled over the town, but there were two lanterns on either side of the oak double doors, and they were lit—which meant there was electricity in the house. She wondered if that was some of the business Garrek had been taking care of in the past few days.

This house had been empty for years, as evidenced by three of the eight first-floor windows being broken. And none of that took precedence over how her hand felt small and yet comfortable in his.

With his free hand, Garrek reached into the front pocket of his pants and pulled out a ring holding three keys. He unlocked the door and let her walk inside first. It was dark for a few seconds, and then the foyer was illuminated.

A grand staircase rose about fifteen feet from the front door. Just like in Gray and Morgan's Victorian, there were rooms on both sides of the staircase, but these rooms were much larger. After closing and locking the door, Garrek led her into the first room on the right. This was the formal living room, complete with a grand fireplace and coffered ceilings. They moved in silence to the other room, her hand still in his. Harper could picture a piano in the far left corner. A couch in the center, a pair of high-backed chairs across from it. These ceilings matched the other room, the floors old and dusty, but of a sturdy wood that would take some grunt work to refurbish.

The tour continued into the parlor and then the kitchen, pantry and dining room. They took the stairs and walked down hallways from one room to the next, ten in total.

When they were in the last room, Garrek finally spoke.

"This is mine now," he said solemnly.

"So what do you want to do with it?" Harper asked.

When he'd first told her about the house that day by the lake, he hadn't gone into any detail. He'd only said that the deed to the house had been transferred to his name one week after his father's death. And because she'd immediately grown excited by his invitation for her to see the house with him, Harper hadn't pressed him with what she now thought was probably a pertinent question.

"What do you want to do with it?" he asked in return.

"Me?"

"Yes. If it were yours, what would you do?"

"I would restore it," she answered without hesitation. "Bring back every beautiful and old-fashioned part of this place and make it just as regal and palatial as it had been."

"Just like that, huh?" he asked and then released her hand.

She missed it immediately. The warmth and the steady feel of someone by her side. She'd never craved such a thing, because she'd never felt it before. Now, in the short span of time she'd been allowed the pleasure, she wanted it back. But she would never say that to him.

Harper shook her head. "I wouldn't question the restoration. But I would plan, meticulously."

She moved away from him then, going to a window seat in the far corner. "I'd definitely need to meet with Mr. Simon to go over the historical preservation requirements. But you've already done that, haven't you?"

He hunched his shoulders. "Nothing detailed. Just the basic legalities," he said in a noncommittal tone.

"What else would you do?"

Harper ignored the sense that he was more interested in her thoughts on his house than he should be. Simply because she would love to get her hands on this place. With that in mind, she decided to answer his question from a professional standpoint.

"I would definitely want to refinish all the wood floors and crown molding. And clean the chandeliers downstairs and in the master bedroom until they sparkled." She ran her hand along the wall that was still covered in a thick wallpaper that had yellowed over the years but still showed the damask print. "I would take my time and make everything just right."

"What if you didn't have the time?" he asked. "What if this wasn't part of your plan?"

Harper jumped then. She'd been staring at the walls and drifting into her own thoughts of restoring this place. She hadn't realized that he'd left the spot where he'd stood near the door to follow her across the room. But the warmth of his breath on her neck and the feel of the front of his body pressing against the back of hers was unmistakable. The quick jolt of lust was intense and rendered her speechless for a few seconds.

"What if tonight was all you had?" he continued, and moved his arms to wrap slowly around her waist.

He pulled her back to him then, one hand flat against her abdomen, the other a little farther up, resting just beneath her breasts.

"If tonight you had to do what you'd been thinking about doing for what seemed like forever. Would you plan meticulously? Do your research? Try to make it great?"

His voice had fallen to a husky whisper, and the temperature in the room had shifted from a pleasant coolness to a strangling heat.

"I'm a disciplined man, Harper. I've had to be. All my life, I've had to walk the straight line." His lips were at her ear, the heat of his breath sending ripples of desire straight down to her toes. "Couldn't do anything wrong in school. Had to get the best grades and move on to a prosperous future. All to keep my mother happy, since my father had broken her heart so completely."

She couldn't speak. Didn't know what to say. As he talked his hands moved. One continued upward to cup her breast, the other moving down until he was kneading her thigh. At her sides, Harper clenched her fingers. She closed her eyes and tried like hell to take a deep, cleansing breath, but it didn't work.

"I cannot do the right thing now. I keep trying and I cannot," he said and then let his tongue run along the outer lobe of her ear. "I cannot..." he whispered again.

"Don't."

This was not why she was here. It was actually the last thing on her mind. Well, no, that wasn't totally correct. Ever since that kiss behind the barn—or, technically, the dream she'd had the first night she'd met him—Harper had wanted to be in this very position. She'd wanted—against all the warnings and the stifling fear—to be in Garrek's arms. To be aroused and taken by this man who had mysteriously walked into town and into her life.

Still, she had to wonder, where was the pain? It always came at this point. The tight clenching in her chest. The shortness of breath. The panic that threatened to choke the life out of her. Where was it?

His hand covered one breast, squeezing until she whimpered. His other hand moved inward, until his finger stroked between her legs.

Harper should have felt light-headed. It's how she'd felt in this situation before. Her heart should be beating rapidly, and her fight-or-flight instinct should be kicking in.

"Don't what? Harper, I need to hear you say it," he continued, this time dragging his tongue to the inside of her ear.

Her knees threatened to buckle, and she clenched her teeth and fingers this time. *Tell him!* The words were screaming in her head. *Tell him to stop and get the hell out of here!*

*No!* a louder voice yelled. *Tell him not to stop. Don't let him stop. Please don't let him…*

"Don't stop, Garrek," she whispered. "Just this once, don't, please."

She was giving him her consent. Once the words were out, Harper moved her hands to rest on each of his, guiding his movements, encouraging them. The feel of his fingers gripping her breast made her feel hot all over. She licked her lips and gasped as both their hands cupped her mound. It was a wanton position, one she'd never imagined herself in, but oh, it felt so good.

He was kissing her neck now, his tongue moving

in circles, leaving a path of moisture along her heated skin. It was quiet except for their breathing, and she thought she should say something. Didn't people normally talk during times like this? During foreplay? Sex talk, maybe? Did she even know how to do that?

It didn't seem to matter to Garrek, because in the next moment he was turning her to face him, cupping her face in his hands and lowering his mouth to hers. Fireworks. Sparks. No, a complete explosion was set off the moment his tongue touched hers. His danced over hers, and hers followed in perfect harmony. Her fingers clenched in the material of his shirt, pulling him closer to her, because for some inexplicable reason, Harper could not get enough.

In the days since their first kiss, she'd branded herself an idiot for reacting so childishly. She was almost thirty years old and should have been able to handle a simple kiss. But as she was being so quickly reminded at this moment, there was nothing simple about Garrek Taylor's kisses.

Now his hands were moving down her sides, pulling at her shirt. She clasped her hands around his neck and arched into his touch. His mouth still ravaged hers as his fingers finally found the bare skin of her torso. Harper moaned the moment those hands cupped both breasts. The sports bra she wore did nothing to protect her from the quick kick of desire as his thumbs moved over her nipples. In fact, that act spurred something so deep and primal inside her, she felt almost animalistic when she nipped at his bottom lip.

It was his turn to moan now and, encouraged by the sound, she sucked his lip into her mouth. He ground his hips into her, letting her feel the persistent growth of his arousal. She wanted it. And him. Now.

It couldn't be that simple. Sex wasn't a simple act. It wasn't something to be taken lightly. It required thought and preparation and…

To hell with that, Harper thought as she lifted her arms and allowed him to pull her shirt up and over her head. This moment was all she needed to concern herself with; it was all that mattered. Not the before or after.

Once her shirt was off, his hands were quickly moving beneath the band of the sports bra. Pushing it up high enough so that his hand could cup one bare breast while his mouth closed over the other. Her modest B cups had always suited her just fine beneath the T-shirts that made up the majority of her wardrobe. Now, she wasn't quite sure they were enough. Until Garrek moaned.

He switched from his hand to his mouth. "I can't stop," he said before taking her nipple between his teeth.

Harper sucked in a breath, her eyes going wide and then slowly closing as the quick jolt of pain, followed swiftly by the flash of pleasure, took over. She exhaled for fear that if she held that breath much longer, she might actually pass out. And that would be a shame. Missing out on the delicious feel of his tongue flicking over one nipple and his thumb moving sensually over another would be something akin to a crime.

"Don't stop," she whispered, her hand holding his head against her breast. "Please, Garrek, don't…"

He did move away then, and Harper couldn't help but feel totally deflated. She lifted her hands and placed them over her face, willing herself not to beg.

"Look at me."

His voice was steely and domineering in the quiet room, and her hands dropped from her face immediately.

In those few moments she'd been cowering, he'd already removed his shirt. Now he was unbuckling the belt at his waist. Her gaze stayed on his hands, watching the light hue of his skin, the long fingers as they moved over the button of his pants, the zipper and then his wallet.

"All you have to do is say no," he told her while he pulled out a condom.

She had a choice.

Her eyes moved up his body to lock on his. He was staring at her. Once again waiting for an answer. She didn't have to think about what she would say.

"I'm saying yes," she whispered and then undid the button of her shorts.

He did not move from the spot where he stood, but instead let his pants and boxers fall around his ankles. His fingers moved over the thick length of his arousal, smoothing the condom into place. It was probably the most erotic thing Harper had ever seen.

"Come here," he said, and the sound of his voice pulled her gaze from his waiting sex up to his face.

Handsome still didn't quite explain him. He was standing there now in the stark light coming from the single bulb in the ceiling of the empty room. His goatee, brows and the hair on his head were so dark, making his skin seem even lighter. And that strong jaw was clenched as he waited for her to do his bidding.

She didn't make him wait long.

She hadn't removed her underwear, hadn't gotten that far when he summoned her. It didn't matter, because the moment she was standing directly in front of him, his fingers were moving along the band of the boy

shorts she wore. He pushed them down past her hips and
Harper did the rest, until she was stepping out of them.
His hands were quick, sliding down her side and then
around to the backs of her thighs.

He lifted her off the floor, and Harper sucked in a
breath as her legs immediately went around his waist.
Then his lips were on hers again, this kiss stealing her
breath as his tongue thrust hungrily into her mouth,
while his hands gripped her waist, settling her over the
crest of his erection.

"Look at me, Harper," he whispered when his lips
finally left hers.

Harper couldn't keep her eyes open. The feel of his
hardness against the most intimate part of her was dis-
tracting to say the least. She wanted to move, to slam
herself down over him and get on to the pleasure she
knew she was in store for, but he held her still. Waiting.

She looked straight into his eyes that had grown
darker with desire. Her hands gripped his shoulders;
her ankles were clasped tightly at his back. They were
really doing this.

"Garrek," she whispered when he still hadn't moved.

"Yes," he said and nodded. "Yes."

He eased her down then, pressing himself into her,
stretching her, awakening her.

"Yes," Harper moaned. "Yes!"

She was deliciously tight.

The feeling that she was milking every ounce of
strength out of him was mesmerizing and, Garrek feared,
possibly addictive. Already, only after a few strokes, he
felt as if he wanted more and more.

He'd already noticed the athletic build of her body,

the long, strong legs and subtle curves. Just looking at her had turned him on, to the point that all Garrek had been able to think about was this moment. The second he could finally sink deep inside her. But after their first kiss, he'd known he was moving much too fast for her. And to his credit, he'd decided to back off, to simply walk away. It was the smartest thing to do, all things considered.

But it hadn't worked. The innocent picnic lunch that was intended to make up for coming on too strong in the first place had eased into an invitation for her to look at the house he'd inherited and to offer input on what he should do with it. Never in a million years would Garrek have imagined that he'd end up drowning inside her at the end of this day.

"Garrek." She whispered his name and nipped at his ear.

Fresh waves of desire poured over him, and his thrusts inside her quickened. There was no other way to describe it, but he loved the moist heat of her tight walls that assisted in his ministrations. She fit so comfortably in his arms. He barely even noticed that there was no furniture in this room. He would ordinarily have never taken her in a place like this, but here, in his arms, it was just too good to resist.

So good that he hated for it to end, but with her legs trembling around him and her blunt-tipped nails pressing into his shoulders, he knew he was lost. With his eyes closed tight to thoughts he didn't want to have right now, Garrek held her close and let go.

It took all of three seconds for him to regret what he'd just done.

Weak.

Irresponsible.

Stupid.

All these words played in his mind over and over again, even as he lifted her slowly off him, keeping his hands on her hips until her feet touched the floor. He wanted to curse. To rid himself of the condom, pull up his pants and walk out of this house. Just as he'd walked out of his apartment in Washington.

There was paper on the floor in a far corner of the room and an unused napkin he'd grabbed earlier at the restaurant when Mr. Simon had spilled some of his strawberry daiquiri. Gray had been drinking a beer and Garrek his favored rum and Coke—with more rum, of course. He could use one of those at this moment, he thought wryly.

With a shake of his head, Garrek cleaned himself up and adjusted his clothes before turning back to face her. He'd heard her moving around and figured she should be dressed by this point. He desperately needed for her to be dressed and ready to walk out of here, out of his life. Because it was a mess, he finally admitted. His life was in shambles and this…coming here to Temptation, and what he'd just done with her, wasn't going to make it any better.

"Uh, well," she said the moment their gazes met. "It was nice of you to show me the house, but I really should get going. If you decide to sell it, just let Gray know. I know some investors who would jump on the chance to purchase and restore this place. So, yeah, I'll just get going now."

She was talking fast and moving to the door at the same time. Garrek felt like an idiot. He knew he should say something. He should stop her. He should act like a man. He wondered if that was something his father would have told him.

He didn't. Instead, he watched her go.

Clenching his teeth and fisting his hands at his sides, he cursed himself. Not only for what had just happened, but for the fact that it had been the second time in a year that he'd sped headlong into a fling, then inevitably crashed and burned. It would appear he hadn't learned his lesson. Instead of using this time away from the career in the military that he'd always wanted to regroup and recover from one colossal mistake, he was certain he'd just walked right into the arms of another.

The fact that this time they had been soft and comforting arms instead of misguided and manipulating ones didn't matter. At the rate Garrek was going, he was likely to lose his job and his self-respect.

## Chapter 7

It might have been too little, too late, but Garrek was finally doing what he'd come to Temptation to do in the first place. For the past four days, he'd been holed up in his room at the B&B, poring over a mountain of papers. Most of them were copies of financial statements and memos that Gray had found in the boxes he'd had shipped to him from their father's office in Syracuse. Others were new documents that Garrek had requested on his own.

None of them told him what had been going through Theodor Taylor's mind in the years leading up to his death.

Garrek hadn't known his father well, mostly due to the fact that he'd been seven years old when Theodor left them, and the visits after that had been few and far between. A small part could be attributed to the fact that

Olivia didn't talk about Theodor much, and neither did his brothers. Gray and Gage had fallen solidly on their mother's side in the demise of the marriage. They hadn't wanted much to do with Theodor when he showed up and weren't as impressed as Garrek found himself when they became teenagers and he realized that his father had taken very good care of them, even if from a distance.

Still, that hadn't brought Garrek any closer to the man. He recalled seeing Theodor at their high school graduation, but not again until Olivia's funeral. Even then, there had been no words. The siblings had all sat together in the front row of the small Baptist church that their mother had attended during her years in Pensacola. Theodor had stood in the back. Afterward, when their father had tried to approach them, Gray had stood between them saying only, "It's over. She's gone. You can go now, too. Again."

The look on Theodor's face had been a cross of shock and sadness, but Garrek thought he was probably the only one to see the latter.

Now, Garrek was here in this town wondering why Theodor had left each of his children a chunk of money and who knew what else. He owed them nothing. He'd paid his child support and then some to Olivia during the years they were apart. He'd also divided his estate and business equally between the siblings. All this extra did not make sense to Garrek.

Neither did what had happened between him and Harper.

He sighed, dropping the papers on the table and rubbing his hands over his face. No matter what he did, his thoughts inevitably returned to her.

He hadn't meant to have sex with her. Not like that.

Not at that time. None of this was supposed to happen. He chuckled wryly as he realized he'd said all of this before.

But he hadn't been able to stay away from her. They'd met purely by circumstances that he had neither planned nor had any control over. Then, as fate dealt another sneaky blow, he learned that she worked for his brother. Temptation was a small town, so there was no way they could avoid running into each other. Still, he could have simply kept it friendly. But he hadn't. The odd pull between them couldn't be explained—or ignored, apparently.

His instinct for handling this new dilemma was pretty much like what had motivated him back in Washington—run far away and forget. This time he could only get as far as his room, which had worked up till now, but the knock on his door said that time had probably come to an end.

Walking to the door, Garrek dreaded who might be on the other side. So far, the only people he'd seen during this hideout were Nana Lou and Otis, the older man who sometimes worked at the front desk of the B&B. From the way the man talked, he did a lot of odd jobs around town. He'd even offered to wash Garrek's rental car, because Garrek had parked it under the huge tree in front of the B&B.

"Birds just love sitting their butts in that pretty black walnut tree. From the looks of your car, they love doing their business there, too," Otis had told him yesterday.

Garrek had shrugged, and after giving the man twenty dollars, thanked him for taking care of the task for him. He hadn't been worried about the car, hadn't even been outside to see it, but if it gave Otis something to do instead of standing at his door trying his best to peer over his shoulder to see what Garrek was doing in his room, and most likely with whom, then so be it.

But it wasn't Otis at the door this time.

"Hey," Garrek said casually after opening it to see his brother standing on the other side once again.

"Hey yourself," Gray replied. "Can I come in?"

"Sure," Garrek answered with a shrug.

He moved to the side and let Gray walk past him before closing and locking the door.

"What's going on with you?" Gray asked the moment they were both standing near the couch.

"Nothing" was Garrek's immediate answer. "How about you? Is Jack's swing getting better? Last time I saw him he was talking about playing for the Orioles or the Nationals one day."

Gray's stoic expression didn't waver. In fact, his brother was now standing with his legs slightly spread, folding his arms over his chest as he continued to stare at Garrek. Years ago Garrek might have been intimidated by Gray's serious look, just as all of his siblings tended to be when Gray was in a mood. All except for Gemma, who always handled her siblings with a firm hand and loving smile.

"Funny you should ask about your family when you're doing your best to ignore us," Gray stated evenly. "And before we go back and forth about this, remember I'm your brother. I know you're holding something back. So when I ask what's going on, I'd like you to cut the crap and give me a straight answer."

And there it was—Gray Taylor, pissed off. It wasn't a sight many got the opportunity to see, because Gray didn't waste his anger on people he didn't care about.

None of the Taylor siblings did. They'd learned to depend on each other in their years growing up in Pensacola. They loved their mother and one another fiercely and knew that through anything and everything, they had each other's backs. So why was Garrek taking a deep, steadying breath and preparing to lie to his brother now?

"Tell me why you're here, Garrek," Gray insisted.

"Because I received your memo and all the other paperwork you sent. I got that envelope just like each one of us did, and I opened it. In addition to the money, he left me a house," he said, feeling a small amount of relief that the words he'd spoken were true.

"Why are you just telling me this?"

"You came here and dealt with his requests to add that wing to the hospital and save the community center on your own. I'm doing the same thing."

"No," Gray said with a shake of his head. "You're hiding. There's a difference."

Garrek turned away from Gray then, because it wasn't easy staring him in the eye and not telling him the truth. It wasn't any easier knowing the truth, either.

So he moved to the table by the window where he'd been set up with his tablet and all the papers.

"A week after he died, this house was deeded to me. The lawyer took care of all the paperwork and put it in a lockbox that went along with that bank account in Grand Cayman. When I closed the account, they sent me the contents of the box," he said.

Then he held the deed out to Gray, who immediately moved closer and took the paper from him.

"This is on the other side of the lake," Gray told him.

"It sits up on that hill, and you can see it from the main road."

Garrek nodded. "I know. I've seen it."

"That's why you asked if we knew anyone from the historical society. I was trying to figure out why Morgan invited Mr. Simon to dinner with us."

"I told her I was interested in some property here," Garrek admitted.

"And she thought you meant to buy for yourself. She was so excited when we got home that night, talking about how great it would be to have you here for good, that Jack and Lily loved having an uncle living this close. Are you planning to move into this house, Garrek?"

"No," he replied instantly. "I don't know what to do with it. If it's a historical landmark like Simon and Harper believe, then I don't just want to sell it to the highest bidder without any regard for what happens to it. So I've been researching and thinking about my next move."

He'd also been thinking about the beautiful woman whose brown eyes had lit up with excitement as she talked about how she would restore the house if it were hers.

Gray looked at Garrek and then back to the paper. His gaze then traveled to the table before he shook his head.

"All of this is not information about this house."

"No. It's about the money Dad left me. I'm trying to figure out where it came from."

Gray dropped the deed on the table and sighed. He rubbed a hand down the back of his head as he stared at all the paperwork.

"I've been trying to figure that out myself. His lawyer read the will. I have a copy of it. We all got everything that was described on that document. All the bank accounts matched the amounts that were initially distributed to us. But then there's the envelopes and the additional money," Gray said.

"What was he doing that he didn't want reported on his financial statements? And why was he doing it? Was it just so he could leave us more money? We didn't need it."

"Guilt," Gray told him. "I've thought about this over and over, and all I can come up with is guilt."

"He took care of his family until the end," Garrek said, even though the words sounded hollow to him.

"He sent checks and gifts and showed up at events, but he didn't have the guts to say what needed to be said."

Garrek ignored the irritated tone in Gray's voice. "What was that? Would we have really heard an apology that was meant for Mom? What was he supposed to say to us, Gray?"

Shaking his head once more, Gray moved away from the table. "You always were his champion. You and Gen always wanted us to welcome him with open arms."

"People deserve forgiveness," he said quietly.

In his mind Garrek was thinking about himself, about how deeply he felt he'd let his mother down and how he prayed each night that she would forgive him.

"Look, I've spent the last few months wondering about this and trying to find an answer. But we all have our own lives to lead, Garrek. You shouldn't be focusing only on this. It's over."

"Is it? I mean, a big part of your life now, Gray, is seeing that all the things Dad had planned for this town are completed. The community center is about to reopen.

The wing at the hospital is coming along, and you're living in the house where we were born. And what about the rest of us? I know what's in my envelope, what he wanted me to have, but what about the others? Whatever Dad wanted us to realize as a result of his last gifts seems far from being realized."

"Your life is far from over, Garrek. So whatever it is that's going on outside Dad's will and this town, you need to realize that," Gray said solemnly. "I'm here for you. No matter what it is, you can tell me."

He'd thought about it. Hadn't he? The night he'd taken the flight into Richmond, then rented a car so he could drive the rest of the way to Temptation, hadn't he wondered what he would say to Gray? And to his other siblings? Yeah, Garrek had thought about it. He'd decided and then changed his mind and then decided once more. This wasn't their problem. It was his. He'd done this to himself, and he would get himself out of it. And they would never have to know how much of an idiot their brother was and how no matter what their mother had said, he'd been destined to fail.

Destined to act in the same irrational and irresponsible way his father had.

This was ridiculous.

And...painful.

"You're going to thank me later," Wendy said the moment Harper walked out of the back room.

She'd worn loose-fitting sweatpants and a tank top to the girls' day out that Morgan had insisted she attend. Now, she wanted nothing more than to lie naked on her bed with a fan blowing cool air directly onto her.

"I'm going to hate you forever," Harper replied instead.

She was walking as slowly as possible, trying her best not to let the still-stinging skin between her legs bother her too much. The effort was futile.

Morgan at least had the decency to cover her mouth as she grinned. Wendy, on the other hand, with her vivacious personality and overwhelming sex appeal, laughed outright.

"No, I promise you, after today, all you'll need is one night in his bed, and both of you will be thanking me," Wendy continued.

Morgan's sister wore red shorts—very short shorts— and a red tank top that dipped extra low in the front. As if her generous cleavage wasn't enough to hate on, she wore three long, thin gold necklaces that each dangled seductively over her display. Wendy's thick black hair was pulled back from her face by a bedazzled headband, while gold bangles jingled each time she moved either of her arms.

Morgan was a little more understated in her pink maternity capris and flaring white top. While Wendy wore red wedge sandals, Morgan had opted for pink flip-flops with huge bows. Harper had rounded out the trio with her fresh-out-of-bed look that included a black tank top with yellow paint splashes on it.

They walked out of Shae's Spa and Salon on Weatherly Street and crossed the parking lot to where Wendy's cute little convertible was parked next to Harper's Ford F-150. Their vehicles said it all—Wendy was clearly the more feminine one, while Harper could change the tires on both vehicles in less than half an hour.

Morgan gasped, and both Harper and Wendy stopped in their tracks.

"What is it?" Harper asked Morgan.

"Are you in labor?" Wendy inquired. "You'd better not be. Not after you've been waxed and buffed to perfection."

Morgan held the lower part of her stomach as she shook her head at her older sister.

"Just kicking," Morgan told them. "These two are going to be kickers for some NFL team, making their dad supremely proud."

Harper touched Morgan's elbow in an effort to hold her steady just in case the next kick sent her off balance. Morgan was shorter than Harper and Wendy, and before she'd grown pregnant with the twins, she'd been a wispy size.

Wendy took her sister's other arm and they continued their trek to the car.

"See, this is why I'm not having any children. Having another human being kicking me is not my idea of fun," Wendy said.

"But lying on a table and letting a very strong woman with a light beard smack oil all over your body, and then cause horrific pain to your most private area, is cause for celebration? You're nuts," Harper told her.

Wendy laughed raucously again.

They came to the passenger side of her car, and she used her key to open the door before they both helped Morgan in. "Look, like I said you're gonna thank me later."

"I doubt that," Harper quipped.

"Okay, well, after your next date with Garrek, I want

to be the first person you call and I want every single detail."

Harper froze.

It was nearing six o'clock in the evening, and the humid late-June day was slowly easing into an only slightly less suffocating evening. Despite the lethargy the heat caused in her, the mention of his name made her heart pound instantly.

"There is no next date with Garrek," she said after swallowing and realizing that her immediate silence made her declaration seem untrue.

Wendy leaned against the car then, folding her arms over her breasts and eliciting clanking from her bracelets. In the passenger seat with the door still open, Morgan even looked up to her with a questioning glare.

"What?" she asked them. "We've never had a first date, so how could there be a next one? Besides, there's nothing going on between us anyway. Dating has never been discussed."

Saying that should have made her feel some kind of way, especially considering what had happened in that house four nights ago. But it didn't, because she'd already accepted that what she and Garrek had done was a mistake. It was a totally satisfying mistake—she recalled the first orgasm she'd ever experienced—but nevertheless one she didn't foresee happening again.

"Oh, honey, please. That date was discussed and paid for in full the night of the Sadie Hawkins dance," Wendy quipped. "He was out at your place the very next night, and I heard from a really reliable source—Andy, who works for you and has always had a crush on me—that he also saved you from being run down by a truck. Seems like some chick-flick scenario to me."

Morgan, whom Harper almost expected to stop them from talking about her brother-in-law behind his back, nodded her agreement. "And he told us that he was meeting you at the Adberry house the other night. So that also classifies as a semidate."

"That was…" Harper trailed off because she was about to say "business," but Garrek hadn't asked her to do any work on the house. Instead, he'd asked her for something else, and she'd readily given it to him. "I mean, we just talked about the house. About what could be done with it."

"And then he went into hiding and you worked yourself so hard even your crew insisted you take today off," Morgan added.

That wasn't true. Yes, her crew had been pretty irritated with her working them for a ten-hour shift on Saturday, but they all had Sunday off so Harper hadn't seen it as such a big deal. And this morning she'd decided to help her dad out at the farm instead of going over to Morgan's house with the rest of the crew. Okay, if she were being brutally honest, her father had asked for her help this morning, after Uncle Giff, Aunt Laura, Marlon and Craig were at the house last night for dinner. Damn those two meddling cousins of hers.

"Look, I'm telling you two honestly that there is nothing going on between me and Garrek," Harper said with what she thought was stark definitiveness.

Morgan looked at Wendy, who returned her sister's gaze and added a shake of her head.

"Wait till he sees the results of today's spa treatment," Wendy told her, "You'll be eating those words, and Garrek—well, honey, he'll be too busy doing something else with his mouth, and his hands and his…"

Harper rolled her eyes at Wendy's crude statement and bade them both a good evening. She pulled out of the parking lot in her truck, thinking how much she hated living in a small town where nothing she did or said could be kept a secret. She was irritated with her family's interference.

And she was driving directly to the B&B where Garrek was staying, because they had to straighten this thing out once and for all.

# Chapter 8

"Harper," Gray said when he opened the door to Garrek's room. "What a surprise to see you here."

He said he was surprised, but the look on his face said he'd been thinking along the same lines as his wife and sister-in-law. That only made Harper angrier.

"I'm here to see Garrek," she said as if that fact wasn't painfully obvious.

"And Garrek is here," Gray replied. "I'm guessing he would like to see you, too."

Harper would say Gray's guess was wrong, because Garrek was standing by the window looking as if she were the absolute last person in the world he wanted to see. His thick brows were furrowed, his strong jaw set and his gaze pierced like a million tiny pricks against her skin. Definitely not the most cheerful welcome she'd ever received.

"What's wrong?" he asked. "Did something happen?"

"Nothing happened," she told him. "I just think we need to talk."

"Interesting," Gray chimed in with a nod.

She'd been so caught up in Garrek's gaze and the strange sound of alarm in his voice that she'd almost forgotten Gray was still there.

"It's about the house, then," Garrek stated as if that were the only thing they could possibly have in common. "You have more ideas about what I can do with the house."

"Right," Gray said with a knowing nod to his brother and then a smile for Harper. "I'll leave you two alone to talk about the house. See you at my place tomorrow, Harper. And Garrek, I'll see you at the community center opening on Wednesday night."

"Yes. I'll be there," Harper answered and then looked to Garrek to see if he would give the same reply.

She was going to the community center reopening the day after tomorrow, but she hadn't thought about whether or not she would see Garrek there.

Gray walked out of the room, quietly closing the door behind him, and Harper's heart began to race. She was alone in Garrek's room with him. They were standing in the living room area, where there was a floral-print couch and a burgundy chair that matched the large rug. All the rooms at the Sunnydale Bed-and-Breakfast had a traditional, old-fashioned feel that matched the vintage Victorian house that had been passed down in the Reed family for generations.

Just beyond the living room furniture was an alcove where a pedestal oak table and four chairs sat facing one of the two bay windows in the front of the house. The table was full of papers, a tablet and a half-empty bottle of water. About seven feet to the right of that table was a queen-size four-poster bed. The one that Garrek slept in.

"I didn't tell anyone," she blurted out, because she really needed to hurry up and get this over with. The quicker she could say her piece and leave this room, the better it would be for them both.

"You didn't tell anyone what?" he asked, still in the original spot where he'd been standing.

"About us—I mean, what happened between us the other night. I went home, and the next day I went to work. I didn't say a word. So whatever is going around town about us is just a rumor. That happens in Temptation. People see other people together and they get the wrong idea. But that doesn't stop them from going on and on about something that's really nothing. You know what I mean?"

His head tilted slightly to the side, but he didn't answer. Which, to Harper, meant he didn't have a clue what she meant.

"What I'm trying to say is that I know we only have a professional relationship—if you've decided that you want me to work on the Adberry house for you. I hadn't heard from you about that, so I'm not sure where that stands. But just so you know, I don't have any thoughts about anything else going on between us."

There, she'd said it. And since he still wasn't moving or saying anything—which was becoming just a little annoying to her—she prepared to turn and leave.

"I wasn't sure what I wanted to do with the house," he finally said when her back was to him. "I'd been thinking about selling it, but I knew I couldn't do that in the condition it's currently in. That's why I asked you to come see it with me."

She turned slowly to face him once more.

"No, if you sell it as is, you'll get only a fraction of what it's really worth. To clarify, you're still likely to get a high price for it. But if you invest the time, energy and, yes, money, to bring it back to its original glamor, your profits will soar."

"I don't have a house," he told her, and then finally, he moved.

He took the few steps from the table to the burgundy chair and sat down with a deep sigh, as if he'd been on his feet all day.

Harper was dressed down as a result of the girls' day-Wendy had invited her to. Garrek was dressed casually enough in shorts and a T-shirt, but even that made him look like some gorgeous athlete. She doubted very seriously that her old sweats and tank top made her look like Beyoncé.

She moved until she was standing behind the sofa, hopefully hiding a good portion of herself from his view.

"I don't own any property, either, but I'm sure Fred Randall can help you when it's time to put the house on the market. His office is down on Carroll Street, right around the corner from city hall. His wife, Millie, is a busybody, but Fred's pretty nice and he's fair. He'll be straight with you about what to expect for the property."

"I meant that I don't have a house to live in," Garrek said as he looked over to her. He leaned forward, letting his elbows rest on his knees, and shook his head. "I'm stationed on Whidbey Island in Washington state. I have navy housing on Seaplane Base. I don't own that."

Harper knew all about military housing. For the first

four years of her life she'd stayed there with her mother and father. Not that she remembered any of that time, but there were pictures, and her father talked about that time fondly. Still, after her mother had passed away, that was the last place Arnold Presley wanted his daughter to be.

"It's an important job you're doing in the military," she said, because she could have sworn it was regret she heard in his voice.

Her father and grandfather had been proud servicemen. Never, not once, did she get the impression that either of them were sorry for the time they'd dedicated to the armed forces. Nor had she ever seen such despair on their faces when they'd talked about their time in the service.

"I know that," he said. "But I should have a home. Gray has a home for his family, and my mother made one for hers."

That was true, she thought. But Harper really didn't know what to say next. This wasn't what she'd come here for, and although she could never forget how it felt to have Garrek buried deep inside her, she really didn't know him all that well as a person.

"I don't know," he said. "Just thinking aloud, I guess."

"That's fine," she told him and moved from behind the couch to come around and sit gingerly on the farthest edge from him. "My dad stayed in base housing with my mom. I think they were happy there." She shrugged. "The pictures made it look that way, at least."

"But you grew up here. In this town and that big farmhouse."

"Yes. I did," she said and tried not to feel too sad about not having her mother anymore. It was an old wound, but every now and then, the feeling of loss could sneak up on her. "One day my dad told me that he'd never wanted me to grow up on the base. That he'd urged my mom to stay Stateside after she had me. But my mother was committed to her marriage and her family."

"She wanted you to stay together," Garrek said. "My mother wanted that for us, too."

"What do you want to do, Garrek? Do you want to live in Temptation or stay in the service?"

She probably shouldn't have asked him that, but he'd opened the door to the discussion, so Harper had literally and figuratively sat down and made herself comfortable with it.

He sat back in the chair then and stared straight ahead. "I thought I knew. Just six months ago, I thought I knew everything. Where I was, why I was there and where I was going."

"But now?"

He shook his head. "I'm not sure."

"Is that why you really came back here?"

"It's why I'm sitting here right now," he said. "I think that's the more important thing."

That was saying a lot, and at the same time, it wasn't saying enough. For the first time since she'd met him, Harper realized that he was just as confused about his life as she often was about hers. That was huge, considering her circumstances. No, Harper was not naive, nor did she think she was the only person in the world with problems, but she did know how hard it was trying to make sense of it all.

"You'll work it out," she told him, because it was what she had to remind herself so often. "Where you belong and what you're supposed to be doing will make itself clear to you when the time is right."

He looked over to her then, his gaze holding hers for the next few seconds—until there was a knock on his door.

Garrek cursed. "Three days of solitude, and the last hour and a half people cannot stop knocking on this door."

He stood as he spoke, so Harper did, too, prepared to leave. She'd said what she came to say, and he obviously wasn't in the mood for company.

"Good evening," Otis said the minute Garrek opened the door. "Got some piping-hot dinner for you two. Was told to bring it right up, as you were both hungry and needed to eat and relax."

"Who told you that?" Garrek asked.

Harper frowned as she tried to figure that out herself. Otis didn't bother to answer. He was too busy pushing a rickety old cart into the room, stopping right behind the couch where Harper had stood just minutes ago.

"How you doing, Ms. Harper?" Otis asked when he glanced over to her.

"I'm well, Mr. Otis. Um, but I don't understand what's going on here," she said, because she wanted to make certain that Garrek did not think this was her doing.

"Just thought you lovebirds would like a little dinner," he answered. "Nana Lou cooked up some of the fresh shrimp her nephew Cyrus caught this morning. And there's some seasoned wedge potatoes fresh outta the grease. Cocktail sauce is on the side, but if you're like me, you'll leave that spicy stuff alone. Shrimp are seasoned just fine, and big ones, too."

He talked as he moved farther into the room, pushing the papers on the table to the side. He walked back to the cart, his bowed legs giving him a wobbly sort of gait, picked up the tray and carried it to the table.

"We didn't order any food," Garrek told him.

"But you gotta eat, right?" Otis asked when he returned to the cart to grab the container of lemonade and a bowl of butter-topped dinner rolls. "I know Ms. Harper does. She had a busy day down at the spa with Wendy and Morgan. I was just coming from down there, fixing those recessed lights in the back room, when I walked in the front door and Mr. Grayson was on his way out."

So Gray had sent him up here with the food. From the way Garrek frowned, Harper could tell he'd connected those dots as well and wasn't terribly happy about it. Neither was she that Otis had just told Garrek where she'd been all day.

"This is Nana Lou's fresh lemonade in the pitcher. Got the pulp and plenty of sugar. It's what they like to call refreshing." Otis laughed then, his high cheekbones and glossy dark brown skin highlighted with the action.

"Thank you, Mr. Otis," she said, because it really was no use blaming him.

If Gray had said something to him about her being up here, then Otis was just doing his job. Just like she suspected Gray was getting used to doing what all the other people of Temptation received so much pleasure from doing—meddling.

"Thank you," Garrek said begrudgingly before walking the older man out.

Harper moved closer to the table, looking at the china plates and folded linen napkins on the tray. There was also a small vase with three fresh carnations stuck inside. Nana Lou kept a huge pot of fresh carnations on the front desk. It was quite a romantic-looking tray of food, if only romance was what was happening here.

"Guess we'd better eat," Garrek said when he came up behind her. "I've learned it's a waste of time to argue with Nana Lou and her cooking."

She was right.

There was nothing going on between them.

There shouldn't be, anyway. What happened at the house was…well, it had happened, but…

Garrek finished his second glass of lemonade as he continued to watch her sitting across the table from him. It wasn't the rum and Coke he'd begun craving again the morning after their night at the house. But strangely enough, he was enjoying it just as much.

When Harper had first showed up here wearing those bulky sweatpants that hung low on her hips and the tight tank top that rode just a little higher than the waistband of her pants, giving him a sneaky little peek at her midriff, he'd known he was in trouble.

Staying away from her had been intended to kill any and all of those eerie little feelings that arose when he was around her. The four-day separation was supposed to make him forget how strong and dominant he felt when his hands spanned her slim waist and lifted her into his arms. How wanted and desired he felt when she let him glide her down over his aching arousal. And that look in her eyes—each and every time he saw her it was the same, like he was the only guy in the room, in the world.

Garrek had never felt that way before. Ever.

It was intense and so different that he figured it had

to be some kind of joke. A cruel and sick one that was bound to blow up in his face any minute now.

"When can you start working on the house?" he asked when he'd decided that thinking about her in any other way besides professional was futile.

He wasn't in the market for a relationship, and Harper Presley was definitely a relationship type of woman. Even if she tried to dispute that fact, Garrek knew differently. She came from a tight-knit family in a town that was full of families, and despite how she sometimes had a far-off, lonely look in her eyes, he sensed she was right where she wanted to be, doing exactly what she wanted to do. Like he'd thought he was doing in Washington.

Now, he had decided that he would hire her to restore the Adberry house, and he would not sell it. At least not yet.

"I'm wrapping up the job at Gray's in the next week. He wants everything done before Morgan delivers. She's due around Labor Day, but really she looks like she's about to pop right now. Ms. Ida says the women in her family never carry a baby right up to the due date, so we're all in agreement that the house needs to be finished before the Fourth of July festivities."

"There are Fourth of July festivities?" he asked, enjoying the way she was folding her napkin.

Her nails were unpainted but still managed to look dainty and neat at the same time.

She smiled, and Garrek felt a quick and potent pain in the center of his chest.

"There are festivities for every calendar holiday, and some made-up ones, in Temptation," she told him.

"I see," he said. "Well, I'll be here at least until then, so when you're ready, we can go back to the house and you can walk me through each room explaining what needs to be done."

"That sounds good. I'll be able to give you a preliminary estimate after that. Thank you," she said. "For this opportunity. I'll do it right."

"I know you will," he said, believing every word.

He'd seen the look in her eyes when they were at the house the first time, and he'd heard the sound of her voice as she spoke about the place. She was connected to that house even though she'd never lived in it, and that's what Garrek thought the place really needed. A connection.

She stood abruptly. "Okay, well, I think it's time for me to go. I've already stayed much longer than I anticipated."

Garrek stood up as well, following her as she moved toward the door.

"Really? What did you anticipate when you came here?"

He'd resolved not to ask her that question. He wasn't going to look at her and wonder how it would feel to have her come here just to see him, to want to slip into that bed with him and let him make slow and passionate love to her.

"I just wanted to set the record straight," she said when she was close enough to reach for the doorknob.

"About what?"

"About us," she replied and then opened the door.

"What about us?"

He moved in quickly, closing the space between them until she was backed against the front of the now wide-open door. Her hands went behind her back, her chin jutting up so that she could stare right at him. Just like that first night she'd looked up at him, capturing him with her naturally beautiful face, her lithe body, her hair and her scent. Garrek inhaled deeply and let the breath out slowly, his lids lowering as he stared down at her.

"There is no us," she said, her voice a breathy whisper as he pressed his body close to hers.

"Are you sure about that?" he asked, putting his palms up on the door on either side of her face, caging her in.

"Yes," she sighed and then licked her lips. "We're not...um, we're not dating or anything like that. Just..." She paused and sucked in a breath as his teeth nipped the line of her jaw. "Just...working together now," she said and cleared her throat.

"I feel like there's something else," Garrek confessed.

He stroked his tongue over the soft skin of her jaw, then moved up to her cheek and over to touch his tongue to the edge of her lips.

"No," she whispered. "I don't think so."

"Why?" He needed to know. "Don't you feel it?"

"I've never experienced this before, so I don't know what it's supposed to feel like," she told him.

He pulled back slightly and gazed into her eyes for several quiet seconds.

"Like this," he said, and then pressed his now swollen erection against her thigh.

She hissed, and her tongue sneaked out to touch her bottom lip once more. He caught it in that second, touching his tongue to hers, making them both moan. Garrek felt her body tense and thought for a moment that she was going to pull away, but then she moaned and leaned in, twirling her tongue around his.

He had to touch her then, bringing his hands down

to cup her face as he took the kiss deeper. This was it, this right here. It was the feeling that he was running toward each time he was near her. Like a sprint to get her and grab her, hold her tightly to him and just sink in. Forever, if he could.

She turned her head then, breaking the contact of their lips and leaving him breathing heavily as he tried to get a grip on his wandering thoughts.

"There's nothing between us," she said again.

She wasn't looking at him at first, but then she took a deep breath and stared at him once more.

"There's this physical pull, I'll admit that," she continued. "But nothing else. Like I said, we aren't dating."

"Is that what you want?" he asked. "You want to go on a date?"

She shook her head and then eased away until she was standing in the hall about three feet from him.

"As far as personal relationships, I've never let myself think about what I want. It just wasn't a priority. But what I do know is that I could never be someone whose only concern is the physical. I'm worth more than that," she said.

Garrek wholeheartedly agreed.

"If that silly auction and the money you paid gave you the wrong impression, I apologize. And I'll gladly give you your money back."

"Wait a minute," he began.

"No. It's okay. I can see how you originally got the wrong idea, and then that day at the house, I didn't make it better. But I'm being clear now. I'm being honest," she said. "There are no hard feelings."

To hell there weren't. He was offended and embarrassed, because as much as he knew he wasn't the type

of guy to pay for sex, he knew at the same time that
he hadn't given her a good idea of what type of guy he
was. He hadn't thought there was a reason to. Until now.

"Harper, you don't understand," he tried to say.

She shook her head. "I do," she told him. "Honestly, I
do. And it's okay. We can just start over. Okay? I'll work
on some ideas, and we'll schedule a time to go look at
the house again."

She was backing farther away from him as she talked,
heading down the hallway away from his room.

"I'll get everything squared away at Gray's place and
then have my crew ready to dive into your project. I
won't let you down in that area. I promise," she said
earnestly.

And then she was gone. Running down the steps until
he couldn't see her anymore. Garrek didn't know how
long he just stood there, staring, wondering what the
hell he'd just done.

Again.

## Chapter 9

Four days later, Garrek had just finished typing a text message and was hitting Send when Morgan opened the front door to let him in.

"Why do you keep knocking on this door like you're a guest?" she asked by way of greeting.

He'd smiled down at her, because in the weeks that he'd known her, she'd begun to sound more like his sisters than he thought she even knew.

"Well, you haven't given me a key yet" was his joking reply as he slipped his cell phone back into his front pants pocket and made his way through the foyer.

The house looked different than it had almost a month ago when Gray had first brought him here to meet his family. The wood floors were newly glossed, as was the dark cherrywood banister leading up the stairway. There were drapes at all the windows, furniture in each room, an array of freshly painted walls, shiny new doorknobs and people. Tonight there were lots of people.

Gray had mentioned that they'd planned an open house because Morgan wanted the town to see the house they'd talked about for so many years. Morgan figured if they just let the people in this time, that might lessen the gossip surrounding the house renovation. Gray wasn't as optimistic about that. He thought the people of Temptation would always be fascinated by the Taylors and interested in whatever they did. Garrek was inclined to agree, since Fred Randall already knew about Garrek owning the Adberry house before Garrek had even asked for his assistance. Apparently, Mr. Simon and Fred were poker buddies.

The brothers had spoken on the phone for about fifteen minutes that morning, during which time Gray had also asked about Garrek's dinner with Harper.

"Sending Otis up here with a tray of food was unnecessary. There's nothing between me and Harper," Garrek had said.

"That's not how I saw it," Gray told him. "And I'm not talking about the gossip. I'm speaking on what I saw personally. Harper Presley is never flustered. She's a candid and compassionate person with a keen eye for construction and a head for business. But every time I, or anyone else, mention your name around her, she blushes. Add that to her showing up at your place dropping the infamous 'we need to talk' line, and I get the picture."

"You've got the wrong picture," Garrek had said. "We're just working together."

"Yeah, you keep telling yourself that. But I know how a man looks at a woman he wants. I was in your shoes not too long ago, little bro," Gray added with a chuckle.

"No, Gray. You've never been in my shoes," Garrek had replied solemnly.

He'd ended the conversation then. He'd also vowed to do whatever Gray asked him from now until he left Temptation as an attempt to keep his older brother from asking about the two things Garrek was not ready to discuss. The first was what happened in Washington and the second was—despite what he or Harper thought— what was currently happening between him and Harper.

The community center reopening had been two days ago, and Garrek had made it through that just fine. In fact, he'd enjoyed standing next to Harper and her grandfather, watching as Morgan cut the huge red ribbon that was stretched across the glass front doors of the building. A wave of something—pride, he thought—had swept through him as he read the name etched over the doorframe: Olivia Lorraine Taylor Community Center.

She would have loved being a part of the town once again. She would have loved her children being a part of Temptation as well. Unfortunately, Garrek didn't think that was going to happen.

Now, Garrek was spending his Friday night at a house party unlike the ones he used to attend when he was in high school. That thought made him smile, just in time for Morgan to turn around and see him.

"Well, I wonder what you could be thinking about to put that kind of smile on your face. Or should I say who?"

His sister-in-law did in fact look as if she were about to pop in an orange dress that barely touched her knees. Around the sleeves were funny little colorful balls that reminded him of the drapes his mother used to have in their dining room. On Morgan they simply looked whimsical, and Garrek thought the outfit suited her perfectly.

"You do know that we're not dating," he said to shut down her not-so-subtle question about his relationship with Harper. He couldn't understand why this topic seemed to fascinate everyone in this town.

"Official dates are underrated. I've been watching you two each time you're together, and there's something there," she told him. She sounded just like Gray had this morning.

Garrek definitely did not want to go there again, and he did not need Morgan to tell him what he already knew. Especially since he hadn't figured out what to do about that situation yet.

"There's also a houseful of people that I'm guessing you want me to mingle with," he said with a nod toward the living room.

"Oh, you Taylor men think you're so smooth," she said with a smile and a slap on his arm. "Come on—Granny gave me strict instructions to send you her way the moment you arrived."

"Now that's a woman I can think about having a relationship with," Garrek said with a chuckle. "She's time enough for everybody in this house."

Morgan nodded. "You've got that right."

They moved past a small group of people Garrek didn't know, but it was obvious they knew who he was, because they immediately stopped talking and stared at him. He gave a nod in return to their inquiring gazes but did not stop walking. Otis was sitting on the end of a very comfortable-looking love seat, his baseball cap hanging on his knee, a glass of punch in hand. He held that glass up as he spoke. "Evenin', Garrek."

"Evening, Otis," Garrek replied.

The man had become one of the steady faces Garrek saw in town, and one of the few people he actually conversed with on a daily basis.

"Hi, Garrek!" a female voice said just before an arm was laced through his. "I thought you were going to stop by the coffee shop to see me."

It was Leah Gensen. Garrek had met her when he was coming from the historical society the other day. She'd walked right up to him and introduced herself, then proceeded to tell him why he really did need her phone number—which she'd coyly written on his hand, and that he'd studiously washed off without committing it to memory or writing it down anywhere. She'd also cornered him at the community center opening when he'd gone to the bar to get drinks for himself, Arnold and Pops Presley—which was what Harper's grandfather had insisted Garrek start calling him.

"I get coffee in my room most mornings" was his reply as he continued to follow Morgan.

His sister-in-law had glanced over her shoulder and rolled her eyes at Leah, who now seemed attached to Garrek's hip.

"That's a shame. We've got the best-flavored coffees in the shop. My aunt even has some original flavors just for our special customers," Leah continued.

"Good customer service goes a long way," he replied, but was already looking ahead to see Ms. Ida Mae Bonet, aka Granny, staring at him with disapproval in her eyes.

"So does being friendly and getting to know the people of the town," Leah continued as if he'd invited her over to start this conversation. "You haven't been getting out enough. I can show you around town. I know you're interested in more than just boring house renovations."

Actually, despite his lifestyle of strict schedules and focus on flight plans and strategies, Garrek was actually getting into the renovation process. In the past few days, he'd discovered that he would need permission to do many things on his property, and he'd begun looking at pictures of southern antebellum homes. He didn't want to seem totally out of the loop when he and Harper sat down to go over ideas for the project. To be honest, he'd been hoping to impress her with his knowledge so he didn't seem like some out-of-touch navy pilot. Her family were veterans, and they still farmed and fit in here. He suspected that's what Harper wanted in her life, someone who fit in with her and her home.

"Nonsense," Ida Mae chimed in. They were close enough that she'd heard Leah's comment. "He doesn't need a guide around a town where he was born. Now, turn him loose, Leah, and go see about your mother, who's probably talking Jerry Bentley's ear off about some fluffy Magnolia Guild business."

Leah immediately dropped her arm from Garrek's and looked as if she wanted to say something in reply to Ida Mae. Instead, Garrek watched as her pert little mouth, dressed in a fire engine–red gloss, puckered and then stretched into a tight line—a version of biting her tongue, he thought.

"Yes, ma'am," she finally managed, but then she turned to Garrek once more. "I'll be around. Don't leave tonight without setting a date with me. For the tour, you know."

Her smile said something totally different. She was a pretty enough woman, with her short and stylish haircut and long black lashes. The purple jumpsuit she wore fit all her very enticing curves, including the snug way it cupped her generous breasts. At another time, in a different place, Garrek might have taken her up on her offer. But not here. Not now. Not after Harper.

"Sometimes the apple sure don't fall far from the tree," Ida Mae continued and patted the cushion on the couch next to her.

It was a nice couch, a rich chocolate-brown sectional. This house was functional. The new furnishings and design were country chic, comfortable and definitely designed with a growing family in mind. That's also how it had felt when he'd lived here as a child. The memory, for the first time in his life, was soothing.

He sat down and leaned in to kiss Ida Mae's cheek. "Good evening, Granny," he said.

"Good evening to you," she replied and offered him a smile.

Ida Mae Bonet was a lovely woman with her creamed-coffee skin tone, high cheekbones and salt-and-pepper hair. She wore wire-framed glasses that made her look sophisticated instead of older, and her lips were also painted a sassy red color. The color matched her feisty personality and highlighted the white linen pants and jacket she wore.

"I see you're getting to know people here in town," she said.

"Yeah, some of them."

"Good. Good," she said and patted him on the knee. "Gotta get out of that room more often. Louise runs a nice little spot over there at Sunnydale, but that ain't all that's in Temptation. You should stop over at the hospital to see the work your brother's doing there. Him and

Morgan are making lots of plans to reach out to the community more. You should be a part of that."

"I don't live here, so I'm a little leery about getting into things I can't commit to long term," he told her.

There wasn't much room for lying or dodging questions where Ida Mae was concerned.

"That's an excuse. I know you got your career—Morgan told me all about that. A military man, that's good and took a lot of commitment from you. But if you'd checked off all the boxes in your life, you wouldn't be here right now," she said.

They were in the living room, where about twenty other people were either standing or sitting, having drinks and chatting. From what he could see, there were also people in the den on the other side of the staircase. Instead of going for the open concept that was popular in homes today, Gray and Morgan had stayed true to the style of this home and kept all the walls in place. So the dining room and kitchen were closed off, but Garrek was sure people were in there as well. It seemed everyone in town wanted to know what this house looked like, as if they hadn't seen it enough when the family had been on television for seven years.

"Don't want to talk about why you're here, huh?" Ida Mae continued when he remained silent.

"I had some time before shipping out to my next post, so I decided to come back here to take care of some business," he told her. He was getting good at telling just enough of the truth to ease the guilt of still holding something back.

But nobody needed to know what life in Washington had really been like for him in the last six months.

They didn't need to know that his entire career was on the line because of one stupid mistake.

"That's what I call fate," Ida Mae said. "Sometimes people get rerouted. They don't always see it as a good thing, but it works out for the best. That's fate lending a hand."

For Garrek, fate was being a cruel and temperamental pain in the ass, threatening everything he'd always wanted in life. Then again, he had learned a little more about the man his father was, and he'd also met Harper as a result of his stay here. What all that meant, he wasn't ready to think too hard about.

"Would you like something to eat or drink?" he said in the hopes of getting her off the subject of him and his life.

"No. I've had some of those finger foods Morgan has in there. I need a real meal, so I sent Wendy back to my place to get the lasagna and garlic bread I baked earlier today. But there's somebody out on the back porch who could probably use a nice cold beverage."

"I don't know that I'm up for more conversation about tours of Temptation," he said with a shake of his head.

Ida Mae waved a hand, the large diamond on her right ring finger catching the light and sparkling. It was an older-looking marquis setting with a worn silver band. Her husband had probably given it to her a long time ago, and she still wore it proudly. The thought made Garrek think of his mother, who had continued to wear her wedding ring on a necklace around her neck until the day she'd died.

"No, not with that silly child. She's over there smiling in Barry's face. He's smart as a whip, and moving up fast down at the bank. I let him talk me into some investments 'cause he's got a gorgeous smile, and last summer he even painted my house," Ida Mae told him. "But you do as I say and take a couple of beers out there to the back porch. Sit down and talk about life and love. That's what it's all about, you know—living your life and finding love."

Garrek wasn't so sure he agreed with Ida Mae's words. Life and love hadn't worked out too well for his family, but he wasn't about to disrespect the woman. So he leaned in to give her another peck on the cheek. This time she patted the other side of his face, holding him to her for a moment.

"Give Temptation a chance," she whispered. "Mark my words, it's worth it."

A few minutes later and two beers in hand, Garrek let Ida Mae's words drift from his mind. That was because Harper was on the back porch, sitting in a white chair with big royal-blue pillows behind her. She was wearing a simple black dress. But as he approached, he realized it wasn't simple at all. It was short. He could tell even though she was sitting down, because there was a lot of bare leg on display. He lifted one of the beer bottles to his lips and took a deep drag. Her shoes were flat but had straps that wrapped around her ankles and up a good portion of her leg. Her hair hung past her shoulders in big fluffy curls.

"Hey," he said.

She looked up at him and a thick lock of that wispy, very feminine hair fell over one eye. His tongue felt thick in his mouth as his body reacted by warming far beyond what the eighty-degree temperature warranted.

"Hi," she replied.

"I heard you might be thirsty," he said, offering her the second beer as he walked closer to where she sat.

"Oh, thank you. I was." She accepted the beer when he reached her. "I just didn't want to go back in there."

To be safe, Garrek sat in a chair across from Harper's. "Yeah, I know what you mean. There are a lot of people in there."

"That's nothing," she said with a shake of her head after taking her first drink of beer. "There's a softball game tonight, so a lot of people are down there cheering on the Temptation Tigers as they play the Bartsville Bobcats. For the last couple of years they've beat us pretty bad."

He sat back in the chair and nodded. She knew everything about what went on in town but still managed to keep her distance from it and the people. Garrek wondered if his mother had ever done that. Probably not—listening to Olivia talk about Temptation, he'd gotten the impression that she was as involved with the town as the town had been with the Taylor sextuplets and their reality show.

"That sounds like fun," he said, even though he couldn't remember the last time he'd been to any type of sporting event.

"I like softball, but people around here can get pretty competitive," she continued.

"You don't seem to like anyone in this town," he said, because he was still trying to figure her out.

"That's not true," she replied after taking another drink of her beer. "I think I just don't have patience for people anymore."

"You've decided that just from living in Temptation? Well, that says a lot about the people here."

"Oh, no," she said. "I don't want you to get the wrong impression about me. I went away to college when I was eighteen, and when I came back I think I was more cynical than I had been before. But that's just me. It's in no way intended to be a reflection on the town."

"Did something happen to make you that way?"

"Well, let's see, I was bullied all through childhood. Seems it's some type of unspoken crime to be a tomboy in Temptation."

"Did you fight back?" he asked, because she did not seem like the type to take any crap from anybody.

She nodded. "Of course I did. Marlon and Craig made sure I knew how to fight just in case boys tried things with me." She shrugged. "They never did, but I was ready just in case. I was ready."

She'd repeated herself and stared off somewhere and Garrek was just about to question her more when they were interrupted. In the seconds before the intruder opened her mouth, Garrek knew this wasn't going to end well.

"Here you are," Leah said, pouting. "I thought you said you were going to come find me before you left."

He hadn't said that, and Leah knew it.

"I'm still here" was his cool response.

Harper had immediately tensed, leaning over to set her half-empty beer bottle on the glass-top coffee table.

"I see," Leah continued and came to stand beside him.

In that moment Garrek was glad that the chair he was sitting in was made for only one person. Otherwise there was no doubt in his mind that Leah would have made herself comfortable beside him. Instead, she looked over to where Harper was still sitting.

"Thanks for keeping him company, Harper. But I'm here now," Leah announced.

Harper stood slowly, and so did Garrek. He had no idea what was going to happen next, but wanted to be ready just in case.

"I see you're still chasing every guy you meet, Leah," Harper stated evenly.

Leah shook her head. "Don't get us mixed up—" she began, but Harper was gone suddenly, leaving Garrek standing, surprised, and Leah looking smug.

## Chapter 10

"Excuse me," Garrek said. "I'm going to leave as well. You have a good night."

Leah grabbed his arm before he could ease past her. Up until this point, Garrek had been trying to be polite. He might have been born in Temptation, but he wasn't one of them. He knew that and respected it. So he didn't question the people here or their ways. His goal in coming here was to keep his head down and do what he needed to do until it was time to go back to his life in Washington. It was that simple.

Now, apparently, Leah Gensen wanted to make it a little more difficult.

"I came out here to be with you," she said to him, her lips once again in that pouty position.

It was a tired look, one he did not like on women who were supposed to be adults.

"I didn't invite you to be anywhere with me," he replied as he stared down at where her hand rested on his arm. He eased that arm away and took a step back from her. "Now I'm going to leave."

"You're going to miss out on a good thing to run after her?" she asked incredulously. "She's not even worth your time."

"I'm going to make sure you didn't offend someone I care about," he replied, and for the second time in his life wondered how someone so pretty on the outside could be so depraved on the inside.

She folded her arms over her chest and pursed her lips this time. "You'll be sorry."

He already was, Garrek thought as he walked away. He was sorry he hadn't realized sooner that he cared for Harper. He'd been so busy doubting what he was doing with her, comparing it to what had happened before, that he hadn't allowed himself to really recognize the difference. He cared about Harper in a way that he'd never cared about Rochelle Ainsley—even now, after all that had happened between them. And definitely much more than he could possibly ever care about Leah Gensen.

"Whoa, where are you running off to so fast?" Gray asked when Garrek bumped into him near the stairs.

"I just gotta go" was his reply as he took another step away from where Gray was standing.

His brother followed him until they were on the sidewalk in front of the house.

"Hold on a sec," Gray said this time, grabbing Garrek's arm similar to the way Leah had.

Garrek looked down at his brother's hand resting on his arm and then up to Gray.

"What's up? Did something happen in there?" Gray asked him.

Garrek shook his head. "No. Nothing I can't handle. I just have to go after her, that's all."

"And by her you mean Harper?"

He nodded, because he wasn't in the mood for Gray's knowing look.

"Okay, yeah. You should take care of that. But I found something that might help us figure out where Dad's other money came from. Stop by here tomorrow so we can talk. I've gotta head out to Miami later next week to take care of some business," Gray said.

He had Garrek's attention with that comment about their father, but Garrek knew he needed to deal with Harper first. "Sure. I'll come by in the morning. Tell Morgan I'm sorry about running out."

"She'll understand," Gray said and clapped Garrek on the shoulder. "A piece of advice before you go. If she's the one, don't let her get away."

Garrek didn't know how to respond to that, so he simply nodded before turning away. He jogged down the street to where he'd parked his rental car. She had at least a ten-minute start on him, but he figured there would only be one place she would go to escape. He didn't really know if she was upset; she'd actually seemed unbothered by Leah's comments. But Garrek knew enough about women to know that appearances weren't always accurate.

He sped the entire way, so he saw the Presley farm coming up on the right side of the road in a little under fifteen minutes. Harper's truck had just pulled in through the front gates and was heading up the winding path toward the house. Garrek pressed on the gas, because he wanted to get to her before she could hide behind the safety of her front door. He might not know where this thing between them was going, or what the thing even was, exactly, but he did know that it was time both of them stopped running from it.

The wheels of his car kicked up dirt as he came to a stop right behind her truck. By then she was getting out and slamming the driver's side door. Garrek yanked the keys from the ignition and stuffed them into his pocket as he got out of the car.

"Harper!" he called to her.

"Go back to the party, Garrek! Have a good time with Leah while you're here. And then go back to Wash—"

Her words were abruptly cut off as Garrek reached out for her, turning her to face him after he'd clasped his fingers around her elbow.

"What do you think you're doing?" she asked when they were facing each other.

"I don't know," he admitted and then lowered his mouth to hers.

This, right here, was what he knew for certain. There had never, in all his thirty years, been sparks like this. The connection was immediately woven the moment their lips touched. That had to mean something.

She balled her hands into fists and pushed against his chest, but her lips parted for him. As if she couldn't fight this any more than he could. Garrek sighed into the kiss, letting the feel of her tongue against his release the tension that had grown since that first night he'd come to this town.

His phone vibrated in his pocket. She was so close to him now she must have felt it, because she used that as an opportunity to pull away from him. She took a step back and pressed the back of her hand to her now-swollen lips. Garrek dragged a hand down the back of his head and struggled to catch his breath.

What had he planned to say to her?

He had no clue.

All he'd known was that he'd had to come after her.

"Leah's an idiot," she said finally, shaking her head and letting her arm fall to her side. "She's been a pain in the butt since elementary school, when I dumped red finger paint in her hair because she wouldn't stop kicking my chair."

Garrek resisted the urge to laugh and shrugged instead. "Well, you said you fought back. I guess that was as good a gesture as any."

"It clearly didn't do the job," she snapped and then sighed. "Still, I shouldn't have said what I did. We can't thumb our noses at the gossip and then feed it at the same time."

"Why don't we stop doing both?" he asked.

When she looked at him again, it was with a question in her eyes.

"Why don't we stop worrying about what other people are thinking or saying and just get on with this," he said.

She looked unsure. "Get on with what?"

They were out in the open. At any moment someone could pull up or come out on the front porch of the house and see them. Garrek wanted privacy.

"Come on," he told her and then grabbed her hand.

The barn was the next closest place to her house, so he walked them down the small incline toward the direction of the barn. She followed, but he was certain she was wondering what he was going to say or do next. For the first time in way too long, Garrek knew exactly what he was going to do and why. He still had no idea how that would impact tomorrow or the days to follow, but he didn't give a damn. Now was all that mattered.

When they were close enough, Garrek pushed on the door of the barn, with the feeling that there was no lock on the door. It creaked as it opened, and Harper followed him. He'd never been inside a real barn before, so he had no idea what to expect. It was dark at first, but Harper moved out of his grasp and switched on the lights.

The space was just as large as it appeared on the outside and, surprisingly, pretty empty. Except for a tractor and a light blue '57 Chevy, there was nothing else inside.

"The chickens, cows and horses are in the other buildings behind the house. We generally just market the eggs and milk and give horse-riding lessons now," she told him.

She looked so small under the thirty-foot-high—minimum—roof and rafters. But he now knew that she was fierce and determined. She was also the sexiest woman he'd ever seen.

"I know we haven't been on a real date," he said as he closed the distance between them. "But that doesn't mean a damn thing."

She'd been standing with her arms at her sides, the tips of her fingers barely reaching the hem of that sexy little black dress. There were red roses on the dress as well—one at her left shoulder, and the other on the right side of the skirt. She reached up and pushed her hair back from her face, tucking the curled strands behind her ears.

"I'm not sure I know what any of this means," she stated quietly.

"I want you, Harper," Garrek said. "I don't know why, because that's not what I came here for. I just know that since that first night when I saw you standing on that stage, I've been drawn to you. I can't seem to keep my hands off you."

With those words he lifted his hand, tracing his fingers along the line of her jaw.

"I don't want to stop touching you. I don't want to stop kissing you. Feeling you," he admitted and eased closer to her, until the tips of her breasts grazed his chest.

Garrek wanted to rip his shirt off immediately. He wanted her bare skin against his own. That's what he needed to feel.

"I just want you," he said once more, leaning in to drop a soft kiss on her forehead, onto one cheek and then the other.

"Garrek. I don't… I can't…"

"What?" he asked, closing his eyes as his hand moved from her chin down to the line of her neck.

He wrapped his other arm around her back and pulled her close to him.

"What can't you do?"

"I can't think," she replied before taking a quick breath. "Whenever you're around, I can't seem to think straight."

"What do you think when you're around me?" Garrek asked just before his tongue traced the line of her lips. "Tell me how I make you feel, Harper. Tell me you want me, too."

Harper didn't know how to say those words.

She'd never said them before, never felt them. Certainly not the way she felt them now. It was in the deepest part of her that the gentle urgings had begun that night of the Sadie Hawkins dance. No, they weren't at all gentle. She recalled her dream and the ache between

her legs that had followed her throughout the next day…
until she'd seen him. When she'd turned around on Gray
and Morgan's porch and seen him standing there, it had
taken all the strength Harper possessed to keep from
running into his arms and begging him to take her right
then and there. That would have been ironic, considering
her past. It would have also been mortifying.

Hadn't she tried to steer clear of him? Sure, her reasons were partly based on fear, but she wasn't going to
split hairs. She could be healed and still worry. She could
tell herself that her past was behind her and that she was
too smart and too strong to let it hinder her growth in the
future. But some days, in some situations, they would
always be just words.

Right here, right now, with this man, those words
were steadily melting away.

She loved how he touched her. Without any fear or
reservation. He simply touched. His fingers moved
lightly over the sensitive skin of her neck, down to graze
the swell of her breasts. His other hand was holding her
so tightly, possessively. She wanted to tell him that he
could have her, that he could hold on to her for as long
as he wanted. Yes, she wanted to give herself completely
to him, without reservation. But fear was a sneaky bas-
tard, and it did not like to comprise.

"I don't do this," she whispered and let her forehead
fall to rest on his chest. "I don't sleep with guys I've only
known for a month. I don't…sleep with different guys."

"I'm only one guy," he replied, lacing his other arm
around her back and hugging her close. "And you're one
woman. You're *the* woman I want."

"It's not forever. I don't know what forever feels like,
Garrek. I don't know what any of this is supposed to be."

"It's supposed to be good for both of us. Pleasure and passion," he whispered and lifted her until he had her cradled in his arms.

She wrapped her arms around his neck and held on. When he stopped at the Chevy, Harper didn't know what to expect. She had certainly never—not in her wildest dreams—thought he would lay her down on the hood of that car and stand over her, staring like he was starving and she was his meal of choice. But that's exactly what he did.

The hood of the car was warm as her bare legs slowly spread open. Garrek's hands were on her knees, pushing them gently apart. Harper leaned back, bracing herself on her elbows, her eyes trained on him.

"Why me?" she asked, wishing like hell she could let those pesky insecurities go, at least at this moment.

He stopped and looked into her eyes.

"I could ask you that same question," he said.

He could, she thought as she stared back at him. There'd always been that look she saw right now in his eyes. The one that said he was uncertain, but that he would forge on regardless. Where Gray was confident and self-assured in business and, it seemed, in his personal life, Garrek Taylor was more reserved, holding back parts of himself that maybe he didn't think anyone else would understand. Harper ached for that part of him.

She also ached for his touch. That's why she reached out now, placing her hand over his.

"I want you, Garrek," she whispered, her voice catching as she said his name. "I want you."

It was permission. It was a revelation. It was perfect, as his hand moved farther up her thigh and Harper felt as if she were guiding it there. When his fingers wrapped around her panties and pulled them down her legs, she lifted up slightly to assist. Then she was sitting up to pull his shirt from his pants. He lifted his arms and she pulled it up and off, flattening her palms on his bare chest. His skin was warm, his pectorals hard.

He lifted the hem of her dress, and Harper moved her arms to mimic his previous movements until the garment was over her head and falling in a heap somewhere on the other side of the car's hood. She hadn't worn a bra because of the thin straps of her dress, and under his passionate perusal her nipples hardened instantly.

She thought he might have mumbled something or groaned, but his hands began moving quickly as he undid his belt and the button on his pants. He reached for his wallet next and found a condom. She watched in anticipation as his pants and boxers fell down and around his ankles, and he once again smoothed the latex over his hard length. It looked magnificent. So much so that Harper's mouth watered, but she knew she wouldn't dare. Or would she?

Her hands would have to suffice for the moment as she reached for him, holding his warm hardness in her palms—thick and stiff, powerful and delicious. The words floated through her mind as she watched her fingers moving over him. She was used to building things, breaking stuff, squeezing tubes and scraping off paint. She was not used to holding a man's arousal in her hand, or wanting to do so much more.

He cupped her breasts then and whispered, "Beautiful."

Harper sucked in a breath. In the next instant, Garrek was pushing her back on the hood of the car. He was moving over her then, taking a turgid nipple into his mouth. She hissed and arched up to him. One hand worked the other breast while he sucked hungrily. Her center throbbed as Harper could think of nothing more than feeding whatever need Garrek had at this moment.

She wanted to scream when he tore his mouth away from her breast to drop kisses down her torso. With one hand still cupping her other breast, he stroked his tongue over her skin, soliciting whimpers and moans from Harper as she closed her eyes to the ecstasy. When he continued to move lower, his hands holding her knees now and spreading her wider, she sucked in a breath and stared up at the rafters. She didn't know where else to look or what else to say. Words didn't seem to come, but she did lift her head to look down and was shocked to see Garrek staring up at her.

His face was inches away from her now cleanly shaved mound. "When?" he asked, his voice gruff with arousal.

"Girls' day," she whispered. "I came to your room afterwards."

He cursed and lowered his head then, tracing his tongue over her skin. Then he was licking, using his tongue to separate her folds and find the jewel that hid inside. He sucked, and Harper moaned.

Her fingers pressed against the hard metal of the car as her legs came up until the heels of her shoes were on the hood as well. Garrek kissed and licked until her thighs trembled and she wanted to scream out his name. Harper bit down on her bottom lip until she was sure she was going to draw blood. Then he pulled his mouth away from her.

He was licking his lips when she opened her eyes and

dared to look at him again. Then he was grasping her hips and pulling her so that she slid down on the car, right onto his waiting arousal. With one smooth thrust he was inside her, and then measured strokes began the torture, all the way in, almost all the way out. In and out, over and over again, until she was moaning and whispering his name. And when she couldn't hold on any longer, Harper let out a long sigh and let the tremors of pleasure completely take over.

Garrek pumped fiercely, like her pleasure had somehow fed the most primal part of him and he needed to find his own release soon. That moment came and so did Garrek, with a powerful thrust and her name on his lips.

"I'm sorry," he said moments later as he backed away from her.

Harper cringed. She quickly scooted off the car, reaching back to grab her dress. "For what?" she asked and hurriedly slipped the dress over her head.

He'd already moved away, turning his back to her. He was adjusting his clothes, and she took that moment to search the ground near the car for her panties. She found them and bent down to pick them up.

"For never being able to wait long enough to get you into a bed," Garrek said and wrapped his arms around her the moment she stood up straight again.

"Oh," she replied. "Well, I think I can do something about that."

He was smiling at her, and Harper felt as if she were glowing from the inside out. In the seconds that she'd thought he was regretting what they'd done—again— she'd felt the icy spikes of fear creep right back into her mind. But apparently she'd been wrong, and she was beyond glad about that.

"Really? What do you have in mind?"

He was still holding her in his arms, rocking them back and forth. She reached behind her back and, with the hand that did not have balled-up panties in them, took his hand.

"You follow me this time," she said.

A few minutes later, when they were just about to take the steps to the front porch of the house, he stopped.

"Are you sure? I mean, your father and grandfather aren't going to be sitting in the living room waiting with a gun ready, are they?"

Harper chuckled at the genuine concern in his voice. Turning to him, she came up on her toes and dropped a quick, loud kiss on his lips. "They're at the softball game. We have the whole house to ourselves."

He smiled then, leaning in to kiss her this time, pulling her bottom lip into his mouth for a quick suckle.

"In that case, a bed might be underrated, but there are so many other great places in a house that we can—"

"Come on," she said and moved out of his grasp.

Harper felt giddy as she ran up the steps. Her purse was still in her truck. She quickly reached into the secret compartment on the side panel beside the door where an extra key was kept. After unlocking the door, she put the key back and welcomed Garrek inside.

He closed the door behind them and then turned to scoop her up into his arms once more.

"Tell me where you want to go and then tell me how to please you…again," he said before kissing her.

This kiss stole her breath, her senses and, Harper feared…her heart.

## Chapter 11

Garrek was surprised to learn that Harper was a pretty sound sleeper. At dawn he was able to slip out of her bed and into the bathroom for a shower. When he returned to the bedroom, she was still asleep. After he'd dressed and she still hadn't stirred, he decided to leave her a note inviting her to dinner. She deserved a real date.

As he'd stood watching her lying so peacefully amid the sheets they'd almost ripped from the mattress last night, he'd thought that Harper Presley deserved so much. Definitely more than he'd given her so far, and more than Garrek had ever considered giving anyone. He had no idea how much time passed as he stood there simply staring at her. But it was long enough to count the twenty-nine freckles that danced over the bridge of her nose, and the circle of twelve that marked her left cheek. And long enough for the thought of waking every morning to this view to sink deep into his mind and, to Garrek's surprise, his soul.

He had just extended a hand, intending to touch her, softly so as not to wake her, one last time before he left. But his phone vibrated in his pocket. He'd been ignoring it all night and decided it was probably smart to look at it now. But not here.

He eased out of her bedroom, being careful to move slowly down the long hallway. There were four closed doors on his way to the steps, two of which he was sure led to her father's and grandfather's bedrooms. In all his years, Garrek had never sneaked out of someone's house. A smile ghosted his lips as he took the steps, thinking there was a first time for everything.

"Just in time for coffee," Pops said the moment Garrek's foot cleared the last step.

Shock rippled through him as he watched the older man set his newspaper down and get up from his recliner.

"Good morning," Garrek said finally, hoping politeness would make this awkward situation a little easier.

"Yeah, I bet it is for you," Pops continued as he moved across the room and through a doorway.

Garrek followed him, slipping his cell phone back into his pocket. He stopped in the big country-style kitchen and took a seat at the light oak table when Pops nodded for him to do so.

"Whatcha take in your coffee?" Pops asked him as he opened and closed white-painted cabinets.

Garrek wasn't a big coffee drinker. His mother used to have a cup every morning. On Mother's Day and Olivia's birthday, Gemma would supervise the boys making her coffee and scrambled eggs for breakfast.

By the time Garrek was thirteen, he'd perfected the heavily creamed and sugared drink that Olivia loved.

"Cream and sugar, sir," Garrek replied as he sat straight up in the chair.

Pops moved through the kitchen, preparing the cups. Garrek looked through the two huge windows on either side of the back door that were open to the early-morning breeze. The sun was up and shining bright while birds flew low and sounds of the other animals on the farm waking echoed through the air. He let his palms fall flat on the table and searched for something to say.

Before anything could come to mind, Pops was back at the table, setting a mug in front of Garrek and one across the wide table where he sat.

"So you're sleeping with my grandbaby," Pops said evenly.

It wasn't a question, which Garrek was thankful for, because he really didn't want to have to answer any.

"I hope that doesn't bother you," he said and sipped his coffee. It didn't taste like his mother's had. Garrek used to taste hers before he would take it to her to make sure it was just right. This wasn't, but then he should probably just be thankful that he was offered coffee instead of being knocked over the head with the mug.

"I apologize if you feel I'm disrespecting your house, sir," he continued when Pops had sat back in his chair and moved his cup to his lips to take a slow sip.

The older man wore wire-rimmed glasses that sat low on his nose. His eyes were a pale gray color that coincidentally matched the short hair on his head. He was a shade or two darker than Harper, and about sixty pounds lighter than his son Arnold. Pops's younger son, Giff, was the smallest of the three Presley men, as Garrek recalled from their meeting at the community center reopening.

"In my day men took their lady friends to the appropriate place to do their courting. Dates where other folk were around to make sure you didn't do anything inappropriate, and motel rooms for when you were inclined to do the inappropriate things anyway." Pops took another sip from his coffee.

The man shook his head and stared down into the cup with a frown. "In all the years my Annie's been gone, I've never been able to get my coffee to taste the way it did when she used to make it."

Garrek took another sip of his coffee as well and then set the cup back on the table. "I haven't had coffee since my mother passed away. After I graduated from the Naval Academy, we had breakfast together at a diner. I ordered us both a cup of coffee, and when they were delivered she fixed them until they tasted just like hers did at home."

He smiled at the memory, because in his mind, he could see his mother smiling as she sipped and swallowed. Damn, he missed her.

"I knew Olivia and Theodor. I knew Olivia's parents, too. They were good people," Pops said. "None of them would have approved of you dropping into town, winning my granddaughter on some cooked-up auction block and then sneaking out of her bedroom at six in the morning."

Well, Garrek thought, that was one way of saying he didn't like what was going on.

"Sir," he began and sat up even straighter. The moment reminded him of another time, when he'd stood at full attention in front of his commanding officer as he looked at him with disapproval, too.

"A soldier doesn't lower himself or his rank by lying. Now you look me in the eye and tell me what it is you plan to do with my granddaughter."

Before Garrek could answer, Pops was holding up a hand, his fingers shaking right along with his head.

"Don't try to BS me. I might be old, but I'm not blind and I'm not stupid. I know you young people see things differently than my generation did. But she's my grand-baby."

Garrek nodded. He understood completely about men and their girls. Specifically navy commanders and their only girls.

He took a deep breath and let it out slowly before re-plying, "I have no intention of hurting Harper. I know the circumstances surrounding us coming together were not ideal. And I do not plan to disrespect her or you again, sir."

Pops let his hand fall to the table. "Does that mean it was one night and now it's over? You really want to tell me that, son?"

Garrek didn't want to tell him anything. What happened between him and Harper was their business. If he had plans for their future, it made sense that she'd be the first one to know about that. Still, this entire situation had always been a disaster waiting to happen. He'd known that from the first time he kissed her. Just as he'd known the night he'd kissed Rochelle in that bar.

On a sigh, Garrek stood but kept eye contact with the older man.

"With all due respect, Mr. Presley, what happens be-tween me and Harper from this point on is our business."

Pops stood, too, moving so fast he knocked his chair down behind him.

"She's my granddaughter!"

"And she's my daughter, Pops," Arnold said.

Garrek turned to see the other man had come into the room. Now this, he hadn't experienced before. Two angry fathers against him.

"What I'm more interested in at the moment is why you're here," Arnold said. "Far as Harper or even your brother knows—because I asked them both—this wasn't a scheduled visit. Now, I know I wasn't a navy guy, but a few of the fellas down at the VA hall were. Winged naval aviators are active duty for eight years. Considering your age and how long it takes to go through the flight training, you maybe got your wings a year or two ago. Which means your eight years aren't over yet. So I gotta wonder what you're doing here."

Arnold Presley was a big guy. He had a dark complexion, a bald head and a way of simply standing that appeared intimidating. But Garrek wasn't intimidated by either of these men. He was, however, growing tired of questions that he couldn't readily answer.

"Exactly," Pops nodded. "So why aren't you on a sub waiting for the call into action, or on a platform training young pilots? You AWOL?"

Garrek cringed at the word that insinuated he had abandoned his commission and his commitment to the United States military. He shook his head immediately, because to do either was never a consideration in his mind.

"No, sir. I'm here to take care of some family business," Garrek replied.

"On approved leave then. Huh?" Arnold pressed. "When is your leave up?"

Again, Garrek didn't have an answer to that question. It depended more on someone else than anything that Garrek could say or do right now.

"If you're asking if I plan to leave the navy and move back to Temptation, I can tell you that answer is no," he said seriously.

That was not his plan, but Garrek was very aware that in the end, the decision might not be his to make.

"Too many unanswered questions," Pops quipped. "When you first walked in here, I liked you right off the bat because you were a fellow soldier. But I don't like secrets."

Garrek was just now realizing that he didn't like secrets, either. Not the one his father had apparently kept about all this extra money he had, and certainly not the one that could end the career he'd worked so hard for.

"I understand, sir. And I can only state once more that it is not my intention to hurt Harper in any way. You have my word on that," he added sincerely.

Even if it meant walking away from her now?

Arnold continued to frown but gave a nod to Garrek. "You can go," he said. "What you and Harper got going is your business. But know that if you, for whatever reason, don't keep your word where my daughter is concerned, this is what you have to deal with. Me and mine—there's three more of us just down the road. I don't care how much money you Taylor kids have—the Presleys are not to be toyed with."

"Yes, sir," Garrek said with a nod. "I hear you loud and clear."

Garrek walked out of the house then, grateful that

the confrontation had gone as well as it had. It could have been much worse. A month ago, the confrontation he'd experienced had gone differently. Speaking of which…his cell phone was vibrating again as he made his way to his car.

He pulled it out of his pocket as he walked and had just opened the door and sat in the driver's seat when he looked down at the screen.

It was Rochelle.

Twenty minutes later, after a tense conversation with Rochelle, Garrek pulled up in front of the B&B. He switched the ignition off and leaned forward to rest his head on the steering wheel.

He'd never felt so alone in his life.

How could someone who had been born within minutes of five other siblings and had lived in a house with those siblings for eighteen years still manage to feel alone? He was in the town where he'd been born and had lived for seven years. Many people here knew his parents and remembered when he and his siblings had been born. There were so many people he could talk to, so many who would perhaps offer their help, or at the very least stand by him while he waded through these murky and unchartered waters he found himself in.

Yet, here he was, alone.

The sound of his phone ringing again made his teeth clench. On a heavy sigh he sat back, letting his head fall against the headrest while the phone rang again. One more time, and he cursed before reaching over to pick it up. There was a moment's relief as he noted who was calling him this time.

"Hello?" he answered in what he hoped was a calm voice.

He was feeling anything but calm at the moment, but knew that it didn't matter. Not right now.

"Hey, stranger. It's so good to hear your voice. Why didn't you tell me you were on leave?"

Garrek leaned back in the seat, once more rubbing his eyes before answering his sister.

"It was a last-minute situation," he told her. "It's great to hear your voice, too."

That was the truth. Of all his siblings, he and Genevieve had always been the closest. Maybe it was his love of planes and of dreaming that one day he would fly off to distant lands, and her creative knack that she would use to add to his dreams of places to go. Whatever it was, anytime Garrek had needed a shoulder while growing up, Gen had been there. And vice versa.

He'd been her voice of reason when she was considering taking a position with a large corporation that would ultimately assume all the credit for her work, instead of taking the leap and branching out on her own. He'd reminded her that they were Taylors and that their mother had always told them to either go big or go home. So five years ago, Gen had started her own company and now made triple the amount of money that company was going to pay her, even designing software for some of that company's former clients.

"You don't do last minute," she said. "What's going on?"

Gen was super smart and intuitive. She knew Garrek better than he thought he knew himself sometimes.

"I opened my envelope from Dad and decided to take care of that sooner rather than later."

"Which is exactly why I haven't opened mine yet," she replied. "But that doesn't answer my question. Is everything all right? Why aren't you getting ready to board that ship and start your new position as department head?"

In all that had been going on, Garrek had forgotten that he'd written to Gen telling her about his promotion and how excited he was to ship out. He'd also forgotten to write her back and tell her the ship had sailed—without him.

"What are you waiting for?" he asked, avoiding her questions about the job. "It's better if we all know what he's given us so we can figure out what was going on with him."

"Gia thinks it's all a waste of time, and I'm inclined to agree with her," Gen said.

"Are you serious? You and Gia don't agree on anything. I mean, seriously, if she says the sun is shining, you say it's raining. You've always disagreed. Why the change now?"

Gen chuckled then. "I know. I know. I was wondering that myself. But the three of us met up last month to celebrate Mom's birthday, and we got to talking."

"Gemma had a celebration for Mom and didn't tell anyone about it? That's unusual."

The only thing Gemma loved more than celebrating birthdays and holidays was celebrating them with the family all together. Especially Olivia's birthday. Gemma always wanted the siblings together to visit the cemetery in Pensacola where they'd buried her, and then to sit around a dinner table remembering all the good times they'd had as children.

"This one was just for the girls. You remember how

Mama liked to select a day where she would spend a few uninterrupted hours with her girls? Well, we all agreed to keep that tradition going, and Gemma thought that weekend was the perfect time to do so. It was great, but I gotta tell you, those infamous envelopes from Dad had us all feeling a little wary."

"Even Gemma?"

Gemma had never let them forget that she loved their father, and she believed Theodor had never stopped loving their mother. She was definitely the romantic of the siblings. Just wait until Garrek told her that Theodor had bought the Adberry house for Olivia, but their mother had died before he could give it to her. Even Garrek had to admit that was romantic.

"She's tired of us all being apart and trying to deal with this. Which is really why I called you. Gray wants us all on the phone for a conference call at eleven this morning."

Garrek had seen the text message from his brother after he'd hung up with Rochelle, but since he'd already been planning to go over to Gray's house this morning, he hadn't thought anything of it.

"All of us?" he asked.

"Yep. The whole gang. Says he got some new information. Must be something big if he wants us all to hear it at once."

Garrek only sighed.

"So once we get that out of the way, I'll expect a return call from you to tell me what's really going on. And don't bother saying nothing, Garrek, because I know better. But I'll give you until after the meeting to get your words together. Now, I've gotta go. I had to move one of my rare Saturday appointments up so I'd be available for

Gray's call. Which is why I'm up at the crack of dawn. Take care of yourself, big brother."

He closed his eyes and realized that the rope he'd been hanging on to for dear life was slowly but surely unraveling.

"You take care, little sis," he said, smiling at their familiar sign-off.

Garrek only sat for another few seconds after Gen's call. The pity party was officially over. He got out of his car and headed up to his room for a shower. But before then, he needed to check in with his captain, William Ainsley. It was past time that they came to terms with whatever Garrek's future now held.

## Chapter 12

Garrek walked down the cobblestoned street as the sun still burned bright in the sky. It was almost six o'clock in the evening, the time he'd asked Harper to meet him, and while the events of his day called for a good stiff drink and plenty of bottles to follow, he found himself needing to see her instead.

He'd decided to walk the five blocks from the B&B to their meeting space across from Treetop Park. There was a fountain in the middle of Broad Street where vibrant-hued flowers surrounded the gated area. Outside the black iron gates, benches circled the structure. On another side of the street were colorful row homes that had stood there since before Garrek had been born. He remembered the houses from when he was younger, because he'd thought they looked like a crayon box. Traffic was directed to go around the fountain with smaller streets they could turn down, but really, the entire area was perfect for picture taking and sitting to watch the beauty that was the town of Temptation.

He walked slower as he realized that someone in one of those colorful houses was responsible for depositing all the money his father had disbursed to his six children.

That was the news Gray had shared this morning with Garrek and their other siblings. Theodor Taylor's additional money had come from Temptation. Who was involved in helping him acquire this money and why, the siblings still had no idea. Garrek had decided at that moment that he wouldn't use any of the money in his new account until this was settled. He wasn't sure why, but he felt like there was more news to come, and he had no idea how he was going to feel about any of it. So he would use his own money for the renovations on the house that now belonged to him. He would restore it to its original beauty with Harper's help.

And there she was. Sitting on the bench with her long legs crossed, talking on the phone. She wore a yellow dress that was much longer than the black one she'd worn last night. Her hair was still curled, but today's sandals had a wedge heel that turned him on instantly. That added height would bring her eye level with him, a thought that for some reason had him ready to see her naked but for those damn shoes. It was an enticing thought—a thought that was helping him let go of the stress of today's phone calls and revelations.

When she saw him, Harper held up a finger. He nodded and sat on the bench beside her. The colorful row of homes was behind him, and he resisted the urge to turn and look at them. To wonder who lived there, and which one of them had helped his father move millions of dollars out of the country.

"I need that delivery to be here by Monday morning," Harper said to whomever she was speaking to on the phone. "You promised delivery yesterday and then this morning. It's still not here."

She drummed her fingers on her knee and shook her head. "No. Tuesday afternoon is not acceptable," she continued. "I'll tell you what, if I have to come all the way up there to pick them up myself, I won't be paying full price for any of these materials."

Garrek thought for sure the person on the phone was about to give in to Harper's demands because nobody wanted to lose money. But then she spoke again.

"Then I'll see you in court!"

Garrek covered the hand that was steadily moving on her knee, and she looked over at him. He reached over and eased the phone from her hand, put it to his ear and said simply, "We'll be there in the morning. So have her materials and a fifty-percent-off the bill ready."

"We will be closed on Sunday," a male voice replied tersely.

"Not this Sunday," Garrek told him. "Be there and have her items ready, or face a lawsuit that could possibly bankrupt your entire business. It's your choice."

There was some mumbling and what sounded like cursing in another language, but the man finally said, "Fine. Tomorrow at nine. Don't be late."

"No. You don't be late, sir. Or it's going to cost you," Garrek told him before ending the call. "You want to tell me what I just said we'd pick up and from where, first thing tomorrow morning?" he asked Harper.

She was staring at him incredulously, and Garrek

kind of felt the same surprise at himself. What had he been thinking, taking that phone from her? He'd been thinking that he didn't like the look on her face while she tried to get what was hers. In essence, he didn't like her unhappy. Not since he'd seen her looking so sad on that stage the first night he'd come into town. His instinct then had been to protect her, and he thought he had. Now, the protective instinct was even stronger. He was going to get her materials and get her a discounted price for them, if he had to fly across the country to do so.

"It was the tile company located just outside Richmond. I've been doing business with them for the last two years, and this is the third time they've either messed up my order or been late. I'm ready to move on to a different supplier, but they were the only one that had the tile Morgan wants in her master bathroom. Once that's finished, the job at Gray's will be complete," she told him and accepted the phone he handed back to her.

Garrek nodded. "Okay, well, I guess we'd better pack a bag and get on the road."

"What? You're serious about going up there?" she asked him. "What about our dinner date? I mean, I can just cancel the whole order and work with Morgan to select something else. I'm sure she'll understand."

"No. We're going to get what Morgan wants. It's just a couple of hours away. We can grab some dinner when we get there, spend the night and pick up the tiles in the morning. The sooner you're finished with Gray's job, the sooner you can start on my…um, the Adberry house. It'll be like an unconventional date."

She sat back on the bench and just stared at him for a moment.

"I'm starting to think everything about us is unconventional," she told him.

"Is that a complaint?" he asked.

Then she moved slowly, coming closer until she'd leaned into him and her face was just inches from his.

"No. Not at all."

Garrek kissed her softly on the lips once, and then pulled back to look into her eyes. She blinked and gave him a small smile. He kissed her again because this right here was what he'd needed all day. *Her.* It was that simple, and then again that complicated. Still, he touched his lips to hers and let them linger.

There were cars passing and probably people staring, but Garrek didn't give a damn. He was kissing Harper because she was what he wanted, what he desperately needed right now. And while he kissed her, Garrek hoped like hell that he wasn't about to make the biggest mistake of his life. Because that's what hurting her would be.

"Thank you," she said when they finally separated. "For everything."

"No," Garrek replied with a shake of his head. He rubbed his thumb over her jaw. "Thank you, Harper."

He needed to thank her for taking his mind off his life in Washington and the mess his one night with Rochelle Ainsley was making of it.

By the time they both stopped to pack overnight bags and finally got on the road in Harper's truck, it was almost eight o'clock. So their dinner ended up being room service in the fourth hotel in Richmond that they'd stopped at, where they'd finally been able to secure a room. Apparently there were two large conventions going on this weekend, so most of the hotels were sold out.

"I'm going to shower and change while we wait for the food," she told Garrek as he sat at the small table by the window, checking his phone for messages.

Under the spray of warm water, Harper let her thoughts wander the way they'd been doing all day. Waking to an empty bed this morning had been a slight blow to her ego, but once she arrived downstairs to interrupt her father and grandfather talking about Garrek, she realized him leaving early might have been the smarter option. That was, until she found out that he hadn't been able to sneak out unnoticed.

"Wait a minute," she'd said as she made her way into the kitchen. "Tell me you didn't stop and interrogate him."

Her father at least had the decency to look like he'd been caught doing something wrong. Pops, on the other hand, had squared his shoulders and lifted his chin. That was his ready-to-be-confronted stance.

"We certainly did," Pops had told her. "And we had every right to, considering he was sneaking around in our house."

Okay, he had a point there.

"I apologize for not telling you that I was having company," she said, and for the first time she'd considered the possibility that it might be time for her to get her own place.

That had never been an issue, because she hadn't dated anyone she'd wanted to bring home with her. In fact, the one person she'd slept with since college hadn't even lived in Temptation, which made their brief affair a lot easier to manage with the men in her family and the prying eyes all around town.

"We're here to protect you, ladybug. You can't blame us for doing what comes natural to people who love and care for you," her father had said.

She was twenty-nine years old, and her father still called her ladybug. He would also still be keeping up with the maintenance of her truck if she hadn't put her foot down about that years ago. It had been hard maintaining a sense of independence in a family full of men who had dedicated their lives to protecting her. Even her aunt Laura had told her it was something Harper was just going to have to get used to. And she had, she realized. In this instance, however, she knew she would have to rethink the boundaries she needed to set between her family and her lover.

Was that what Garrek was? Her lover? Or was he more? Did he want more? All these questions had rambled in her mind as her father and grandfather continued to stare at her.

"He's important to me," she'd admitted to them.

"We know that," Arnold said. "Or he wouldn't have been in this house by your invitation. We just want to make sure he's worthy."

She shook her head at him. "That's not your call."

But she did understand what he was saying. If she had an only child that she'd spent years away from because of her job, she would be overprotective, too.

Harper had taken a deep breath then and looked at the two men she'd spent all her life loving completely. They were the only men she'd ever given that emotion to, and the only men who had returned it.

"I don't know why he came back to Temptation, and

to be honest, I haven't pressed him for details. I've simply been trying to enjoy the fact that he is here."

*And that he seems to be really interested in me.*

"Honor. Respect. Loyalty," Arnold said. "We Presleys pride ourselves on that. If he's the one for you,
ladybug, you just make sure that he has those qualities.
You make sure that his heart is with you if you plan to
give him yours."

She'd told her father that she understood what he was
saying, and then she'd returned to her room. But as she
moved through her day, she'd been torn between the part
of her that was eager to see Garrek again and the part
that knew her father and grandfather were right. She
did need to know what Garrek was really doing back in
Temptation. She also wanted to know what his future
plans were. Was he staying in Temptation or returning
to the navy? And more importantly, where did either of
those decisions leave her?

After running some errands, Harper had done something else she'd never figured she would do. She'd called
Wendy for help.

"I just want to look good for this date," she'd said.

Wendy had been elated. "Oh, yes, honey!" she'd
squealed. "I thought you did a good job with your hair
last night, and that dress was nice, but it's time to really
knock him off his feet."

It had sounded like too much, and Harper had instantly tried to back out, but Wendy wasn't having it.
She'd been at the farm at four o'clock and had spent the
next hour and a half doing all sorts of girly things to
Harper. From plucking her eyebrows in the most painful fashion ever to insisting on a new color of polish
for Harper's fingers and toes, it took forever just to get

dressed, but when she was and Wendy had pushed her in front of the mirror, Harper had been pleased. She not only looked like an attractive woman, she also felt like one in the billowy butter-yellow dress. The thin straps and low neckline made cleavage that Harper never knew she possessed appear. And when she added the shoes, the height that she felt like she'd always been plagued with seemed elegant and sexy.

She'd thanked Wendy with hugs and kisses and a promise to pay her back before driving to the meeting place Garrek had designated in his note to her. A note that she'd found sweet and had tucked away to save. It was when she'd been waiting for Garrek that they had called her to report the missing tile. The interruption had irritated her, until Garrek had come in and made it all better. Just as he had that night at the dance.

Now, they were in this hotel preparing to spend another night together. She should be excited for this next step in their relationship. It was a relationship, right? Was that what she wanted?

She stepped out of the shower, shaking her head at all the questions that just did not seem to quit. She thought Wendy would undoubtedly lose her mind if she found out all the glam work she'd done had been for nothing. She and Garrek hadn't gone out to a public dinner; instead he was about to see her in the daintiest nightgown she owned—a T-strap cotton item that came to just above her knees. The only other option was the outfit she'd packed for tomorrow—jeans and a T-shirt. So she'd shrugged and dressed and then prepared to go out into the other room and ask the questions she needed answers to.

The two white candles, lit and sitting in the center of

that little table, stopped her cold. The food had arrived, and Garrek had set the table with plates and glasses. He still wore the dark blue pants and lighter blue shirt he'd had on earlier, and he still looked as dashing as he had the first night she'd met him. Suddenly she felt under-dressed and out of place.

"You're lovely," he said and extended a hand to her.

Okay, well, that made her feel better. How did he always manage to do that?

"All this for chicken tenders and French fries?" she asked as she approached the table.

That's what she'd ordered because there hadn't been anything else on the menu that she'd wanted to eat at this time of night.

"No. All of this is for you," he told her.

Butterflies fluttered in her stomach as she sat down. Harper smiled nervously and then thought she was being terribly silly. This wasn't the first time she'd been alone with Garrek. It wasn't even the first night she would be spending with him. So why did this all seem so different from any other interaction they'd ever had?

"You're really good with women," she said when he finished moving their food from the cart to the table. "That's one of the rumors flying around town that I guess I can attest to."

"Don't believe everything you hear," he said as he opened honey barbecue sauce.

"Those are certainly words to live by," she said. "Still, I would be lying if I didn't admit that I've wondered why you're single."

He looked up and stared without speaking for longer than she was comfortable with. Then he resumed preparing his food before saying, "I wasn't involved with anyone when I came to Temptation."

"Neither was I," she said to mask the wave of relief that washed over her.

"If you had been, I'd want to personally kick the guy's ass for allowing you to be auctioned off."

She'd almost forgotten about that.

"I didn't know that's what they were going to do."

"I know you didn't."

"And I didn't need anyone to get me a date."

He nodded. "I know that, too."

"Do you?" she asked. "How?"

He already had a few fries in his mouth, and waited until he finished chewing to reply. "You're an attractive woman. No, don't look at me like that. You are. But you have a very quiet appeal that is like a sucker punch the second a guy really looks at you."

"Is that what you did?" she asked while absently arranging the food on her plate. "You really looked at me?"

"No," he answered. "They made the announcement that I was the highest bidder, and I was dragged onto that stage. But the moment I saw you…let's just say the hazy fog of the drink I'd just downed cleared instantly."

She smiled at that. "I didn't expect you—or anyone, for that matter—to bid."

"Don't tell me you don't think you were good enough for any guy in that room, or we're going to have a long conversation about that."

"No," she said and shook her head. "Not that. I don't have self-esteem problems. At least, I don't think I do anymore. I just came to some conclusions about myself a long time ago. And about the people in Temptation."

"I'm not concerned with the people of the town," he

said and took a sip of his water. "I want to know what conclusions you came to about yourself."

She chewed on an unappealing French fry. "It's not important."

"It is, because you're important," he said. "To me, you're very important."

Again with the butterflies. Harper had to clear her throat to be sure she didn't ramble when she spoke again.

"I know I'm not like most women. I figured that out when I was twelve and everyone around me started to get boobs and butts and I continued to look like Craig and Marlon, straight up and down and skinny as a pole."

"I think your body is beautiful," he told her, his voice lowering just a bit as he spoke.

Heat fused her cheeks, and those butterflies did an entire step routine in the pit of her stomach at his words. Then something else happened. Something that Harper would never be able to explain. But beneath his genuine gaze and amid all that she'd learned about herself in these past weeks, she felt emboldened and as strong and independent as she had always tried to be. This feeling she had right now had always eluded her.

"Wow, I wish you would have stayed in Temptation," she said with a nervous chuckle. "I carried those insecurities with me all the way to college. I went from being bullied by Leah and her crew to my roommate, Nancy, and her band of merry witches."

Harper picked up her napkin then. She unfolded it and seconds later started to fold it again.

"Nancy and her crew assumed I was a lesbian because I didn't dress or act like them, and I wasn't obsessed with makeup like they were. When I was thirteen I spent the weekend at my uncle Giff's house. I snuck into Aunt

Laura's makeup box and tried to hide my freckles with her Mary Kay products. Two hours later, in addition to the freckles, I had red splotches all over my face. It itched and burned, and I thought I was going to die." She shrugged at the memory. "Turns out I was allergic to something in the makeup, and after the doctor gave me a good dose of Benadryl, Aunt Laura explained to me that I had sensitive skin and that maybe I needed to use more natural-based beauty products. I never did, though," she said and looked up from the napkin to see that Garrek was staring intently at her now.

She took a deep breath and decided she was all in now. After releasing the breath slowly, Harper continued.

"In college I wore my hair in two braids or a pony-tail because they were the only styles I could manage. I was never very interested in hair and clothes while growing up in Temptation. My dad sent money home for my care, and Pops always gave some to Aunt Laura to handle all my "girly needs" as he used to call them for me. So she bought me pretty dresses to wear to church on Sundays, but on the other days she understood that I preferred jeans and shorts to skirts and frilly tops. She might have been the only woman in town to ever un-derstand that about me. Anyway, Nancy and her crew made their judgment of me about ten minutes after I moved into the dorm. After the first time I stood up to them—the night of some frat party I refused to attend—they decided I was beneath them. I didn't care at first because I went to school to learn, not to make friends. I'd decided a long time ago that I didn't need friends, because I had my family."

"You needed to be treated fairly," Garrek said.

Harper was grateful for his interruption because emotion was swelling in her chest. The buildup to what she ultimately wanted to tell him was real; the anxiety about how he was going to react when she said it was terrifying. All because she'd gone and done something she'd never thought she would do.

She'd fallen in love.

Willing her fingers to stop moving over the napkin that she'd now folded and unfolded three times, Harper shook her head and squared her shoulders. She looked directly at him and knew what had to be done.

"The end of my junior year, I was so tired of the whispers and the insults that I just agreed to go to one of the year-end parties. I let Nancy pick out a dress for me, and one of her cronies did my hair and makeup. I stood on the patio of the house where the party was held for the first forty-five minutes I was there. Then he appeared."

She bit her bottom lip and then clasped her hands in her lap and cleared her throat.

"He played football and was wearing his jersey. He was cute and I was probably tipsy." She stopped and then shook her head. "No. I wasn't. I'd nursed that one glass of spiked punch since it had been slipped into my hand two minutes after I walked into the party. I could taste the liquor in it, but I hadn't drunk enough to feel any different than I had when I arrived."

Garrek waited for her to continue.

"His name was Len. Leonard Ruffin III. He said he liked my hair, and he invited me upstairs to his room where it was quiet. I went because he was a football player and he'd noticed me out of a houseful of other girls. I thought, *So this is how it feels to like a boy.* I'd never felt that before, so I assumed it was a good thing.

"It was all a joke," she said, feeling her heartbeat

quicken. "The minute he closed the door to his room, he was on me. Kissing me, touching me, pushing me toward the bed. I told him to stop, more than once. At least ten times, I'm sure. That's how many times it took to really piss me off. That's when I recalled everything Marlon and Craig had ever taught me, and I kneed Len in the balls. He was on top of me at that point and I was struggling to get off that bed, so it wasn't with as much force as I intended. It didn't stop him for long. My hair was no longer pretty. I was now the teasing slut. He came after me again, but this time I was ready. I kicked him in the groin and jumped up the moment he stumbled back. As he was going down on his knees I punched him in the face. Blood splattered everywhere. He yelled and I kicked him until he fell flat on his back."

"Good for you," Garrek said tightly.

Harper shook her head again, one tear slipping down her cheek. She hurriedly wiped it away and tried to smile. "His friends kicked down the door and held me while they called campus police. They took me out of the house and to their security office on campus. I was held there until late the next afternoon, when I was told Len and his family had decided not to press assault charges against me. When I told them that he'd sexually assaulted me, they laughed and advised I take the Ruffins' generosity as a gift and finish my last year in silence."

Another tear threatened to fall, but Harper blinked to hold it back. She stood and turned away from Garrek because this was much harder than she ever thought it would be.

"I came home to Temptation for the summer, worked on the farm and built a new chicken coop for my dad, because he'd strained his shoulder while trying to wrangle one of the horses into the stable during a thunderstorm. I painted my bedroom and bought my first truck with the money I'd made tutoring throughout the school year. In August I packed up my bags and drove back to school. I finished my senior year, graduating in the top five percent of my class. I came back to Temptation and accepted an internship with the Yankin Group, one of the largest construction companies on the East Coast. I eventually accepted a job offer as project manager with them and stayed for three years. I was ready for my own company by then, so I came back to Temptation and opened Presley Construction."

"And you never told anyone else about what happened with Ruffin, did you?" he asked.

Harper could only shake her head in response. This was something that she'd carried for the last seven years. It was her experience, in essence her introduction to the real world. So no, she hadn't shared it with anyone, not even her father. Especially not her father. And it wasn't that she was ashamed of what had happened. She knew it wasn't her fault. But the thought of bringing even more negative attention to herself—after enduring the taunts and disrespect for the majority of her life—had been too much to bear. She knew that it was probably cowardly on her part, but she'd taken the road that was easiest for her to make it through.

"I decided not to file another report after telling the security officers that first night. Len's father was a college football coach. Somewhere on the West Coast, I think. But he had pull in the collegiate world. His son was probably going to go on to play in the NFL. I was the skinny, unattractive girl from a town called Temptation. I already knew what the outcome was going to be," she said.

Now, all these years later, she wished she'd been as strong as she felt right now.

Harper jumped when his hands touched her shoulders, but she settled immediately as he pulled her back to him. Harper felt his strength as if it were literally oozing from him and pouring into her. When he leaned in and kissed her hair while wrapping his arms around her, she felt his compassion and melted into the comfort.

"You are beautiful," he whispered. "And strong. And smart. I am honored to know you, to know all of you, Harper Presley."

Harper turned in his arms then. She wrapped her arms around him and buried her face in his chest, breathing all the years of fear and regret she'd felt into him. Tears spilled from her eyes, and she didn't try to stop them. She just let them fall. And Garrek held her while she did so.

She had no idea when he carried her to the bed and lay down beside her, because the tears had still been flowing. She'd still been purging herself of the darkest time in her life, the lowest she'd ever felt—and the moment she knew it was time to let it go.

## Chapter 13

Garrek woke with a start.

His quick movement had Harper shifting in his arms, reminding him that he hadn't been sleeping alone. Staring down at the top of her head, he remembered what she'd told him last night, the thought making him hug her closer. She had one leg twisted between his, her head on his chest, her arm around his waist. Garrek rubbed one hand over her back and the other down her hair as he kissed the top of her head. When she snuggled closer to him, guilt threatened to choke him.

He closed his eyes to the constricting sensation in the hope of some relief. It didn't work. Closing his eyes only brought back the dream he'd just had. The one where he'd turned into his father.

His mother had sat in her favorite rocking chair on the back porch of their Pensacola Bay home. The house was an old Cape Cod–style dwelling surrounded by Spanish moss–laden oak trees. It had been built in 1928 and had four bedrooms and four bathrooms. The back porch was enclosed by a screen and looked directly out onto the bay. Olivia would often sit there with her cup of coffee just before dawn.

In his dream Garrek had been sitting there with her, a cup of coffee in hand, too. He'd sipped and smiled at the familiar taste.

"You need to tell her," Olivia had said after they'd sat in silence for a few minutes.

Garrek had lowered his cup, still holding it in both hands as he stared out at the water. The first burnt-orange rays of impending sunlight had begun to shimmer over the horizon.

"If you plan to give her your heart, you need to start with honesty," she continued.

"I didn't plan any of this," he replied.

"That's how it is sometimes," she said and took another sip from her cup. "We make plans and He changes them." She chuckled.

Garrek felt his heart clench at the memory of the sound.

"I used to laugh when my grandmother told me that, but now I know. I didn't plan for this, and yet I've been able to find some happiness here in Florida. Some peace. And me," she said wistfully. "I found me down here, away from your father."

"I don't want what the two of you had." Garrek said what had been on his mind for years.

He'd never wanted to fall in love with someone and give them the power to rip out his soul when they left. It wasn't an option for him.

"We had six beautiful blessings," Olivia told him. "For those reasons alone, I would do everything with Theodor over again without a second thought."

Garrek did not speak.

"You'll miss the bigger blessing if you keep trying to play it safe. You're falling in love with this woman and she's falling in love with you. She told you about her painful past. Now it's time for you to tell her about yours."

"Before it's too late." Theodor's voice had interrupted the quiet morning on the porch with his mother.

When Garrek turned in his rocking chair, it was to see his father lying in his casket, hands folded over his chest, eyes wide-open.

"I waited too long to admit that I still loved your mother. I wanted to show her and prayed she would take me back when she saw the house. But I took too long and she left here without me ever telling her," Theodor said.

Garrek stood from the rocking chair and moved closer to the casket. The warm summer morning that had accompanied his conversation with his mother changed to a cool breeze, and he turned back to see that Olivia and her prized view of the bay had disappeared. There was only this sterling-white room now, with the charcoal-gray casket where his father lay.

"Don't make my mistakes," Theodor said. "Be a better man than I could."

"The money," Garrek said. "Where did you get that money?"

Theodor hesitated, and Garrek moved closer until he could clench his fingers on the side of the casket.

"Tell me where you got the money!" he insisted.

"Tell her!" Theodor said. "Tell her that you love

her and that the past will not predict your future. Tell her now!"

The white room went completely dark, and Garrek was instantly alone.

That's when he'd awakened, fearing that he would always be alone.

The feeling of Harper's hand moving over his lower abdomen yanked him firmly into the here and now, and he blinked to clear his thoughts.

Her hand moved farther down, pushing past the elastic band of his boxers. Sometime during the night he'd gotten up and taken off his clothes. Harper had cried for a while, and then they both must have dozed off while he'd been still dressed. Now, her bare leg was moving slowly down his and her hand… He sucked in a breath as her fingers closed over his awakening length.

She didn't speak, and Garrek was rendered speechless as her ministrations continued. While one hand moved, bringing him completely back from his dream state, her other hand pushed his boxers farther down his thighs. He helped by lifting up and then kicking them off the rest of the way as she moved between his legs.

Garrek looked down at her tousled hair and ran his hands through the soft strands, pushing them back. He wanted to see her face. She looked up then, both her hands moving over him now. Her eyes were a gorgeous shade of brown, like a cold glass of root beer. She had long lashes and a pert little nose. She also had high cheekbones and freckles and a pretty tongue that was now snaking out from between her lips. She continued to watch him watching her as she lowered her face close to her hands, her tongue touching the tip of his erection.

Garrek sucked in a breath a moment before her tongue

stroked him once more, and then her mouth opened to take him inside. She moved slowly, tentatively—expertly, in his opinion. His eyes closed involuntarily, and his fingers clenched in her hair.

What was she doing to him?

Killing him, that was what. Slowly but surely Harper Presley was killing the man Garrek once thought he was, and awakening someone he'd never dreamed he'd be.

With each up and down movement, each languid lick of her tongue, she was tearing him apart. He wanted her to stop, wanted this whirlwind that he felt his life had been to slow down and let him catch his breath. But it didn't. She didn't, and he did nothing to try to make her. In fact, his hands were now guiding her head, his hips pumping slowly in sync with her movements.

It was heaven. A glimpse of what sheer bliss could be. Her mouth was so hot, her hair so soft, face so pretty. This was a perfect beginning to a day. And if he didn't stop her soon, it was going to be a perfect ending—for him at least.

Garrek gently nudged her head so that her mouth eventually released him. He rolled off the bed and fumbled with his pants to find his wallet and a condom, rolling it on faster than he ever recalled in his life. Harper was on her knees, watching and waiting, so that when he climbed back on the bed she quickly pushed him down on the mattress.

She was on top of him before he could speak, her legs straddling his waist. He reached up to touch her then, pushing her nightshirt up over her hips while she once again wrapped her fingers around his length. Garrek lowered her over his arousal, groaning as first his tip slipped in, and then every inch in the most excruciating pleasure he could have ever imagined.

Harper began moving immediately, riding him until dreams, confessions—hell, even his name—vanished from his mind. There was only her now. Her measured thrusts and slim fingers that scraped along his thighs and between his legs as she cupped his sac. Garrek gripped the sheets in an effort to hold on. It was futile, because the more she moved, the louder her little moans grew, and the instant her thighs clenched and her body began to tremble, he knew he was lost.

Done.

Complete.

Finished.

And dangerously close to admitting he was in love with this woman.

This was Harper's first time showering with a man. Actually, this morning had been the first time she'd done a couple of things. The smile that ghosted her face as she stood beneath the shower spray said she wasn't displeased by any of them. The way Garrek was slowly dragging the soaped cloth over her back, down and over the curve of her bottom and lower, said he was pretty pleased with her first endeavors as well.

"Now the front," he said, and Harper turned to face him.

"I don't know how we would get anything done if this was an every-morning ritual," she joked.

His reaction was quick—the hesitation like a knife to her skin. To his credit, Garrek rebounded just as fast. He smiled at her and continued to move the cloth over her body. He took his time, not missing one inch of her, and soon she forgot to be hurt by his momentary rebuff.

It wasn't until after their shower, when they returned to the room wrapped in towels, that her conscience insisted she press forward. She'd told Garrek a lot about herself last night. Things that she'd never told anyone before. In the light of a new day, she realized she needed to know a little about his past life as well.

"I know that Gray didn't plan on staying in Temptation when he came back, but now he has a family there," she started as she moved to her bag. "What are your plans, Garrek? Are you staying in Temptation?"

Straight to the point. That was the only route she could afford to take. She was invested in this relationship now. She'd given of herself physically and emotionally, and if she were going to take another step forward, she had to have full disclosure. Garrek was keeping something from her, and possibly from his family, too. She wanted to know what it was.

"That's not why I came back" was his response.

When she turned, it was to see that he was once again staring down at his phone.

"You came back because your father left you a house," she said. "You've decided to restore that house but don't know if you'll sell it or keep it. But you have to be thinking of what comes next. What about your career in the navy? How is that affected by your father's gift to you?"

He looked up from the phone to stare at her.

The white hotel towel was wrapped around his waist. His chest was bare, muscled and mouthwatering. Harper gripped the clothes she'd pulled out of her bag and dragged her gaze back up to his face.

"I don't know what comes next," he replied. "Honestly, when I came to Temptation, it was with one thought in mind—to bury myself in the business of handling the things my father left for me."

"And now?" she asked. "Are you still not thinking about what comes next?"

He reached down for his bag and lifted it. "If your real question is, am I thinking about what comes next with you, the answer is yes. I haven't been able to stop thinking about that."

Now, that was what she wanted to hear. Wasn't it? She wasn't sure. Or rather, she was certain she felt relieved and excited by the fact that he was thinking of her with a future in mind. Still, she couldn't shake the feeling that there was so much more going on with him than just the house and her. More that he apparently did not trust her enough to share.

"I'm gonna go get dressed so we can head out. We don't want to be late and give that idiot at the tile shop any ammunition to stiff you on your product," Garrek told her.

Without waiting for a response, he took his bag and headed back into the bathroom. Harper hurriedly slipped into her clothes and packed. She was heading back to the nightstand to get her phone and charger when a vibrating sound came from it before she could reach it.

As she came closer to the nightstand, she could see that it wasn't her phone that was vibrating. Garrek's was charging right beside hers, and the screen on his phone was lit up as the text message came through. She hadn't meant to…it wasn't something she would ever do— invading someone else's privacy was a no-no. And especially since it was a man she was sleeping with. Hadn't she just been thinking about how he couldn't possibly trust her? Hadn't she just been wondering...

Harper's breath caught as she read the message, despite her resolutions not to.

The prenatal paternity test results are in. Call me ASAP. Rochelle

The moment Garrek stepped out of the bathroom, he knew something was very wrong.

As he'd closed himself in the bathroom minutes before, he'd known something was off. Harper had questions about him. Her family had questions about him. His family had questions. It was past time he started answering them and dealing with the repercussions as they came.

He was not prepared to find Harper gone.

But as he moved through the room looking for her purse or her overnight bag, he saw neither. Maybe she'd gone down to the truck to wait for him. They were running a little behind as a result of their early-morning lovemaking and the long, delightful shower. After making sure he had everything in his bag, he decided that was it; she was waiting in the truck. He would just give her a call to let her know he was on his way down.

His phone rang, and Garrek cursed as he answered it.

"Yes?" he yelled, as the feeling that something was wrong intensified.

"Where are you?" Gray asked, his voice sounding just as strained as Garrek's.

"I'm in Richmond. Why? What's wrong?"

"The navy masters-at-arms just left my house," Gray said tightly. "Two of them knocked on the door at eight a.m., and when I let them in, they said they were looking for you."

Garrek cursed and sat down heavily on the bed. "I can explain," he said.

"I know you can, and I won't waste time by saying you should have explained what the hell was going on the second you stepped foot in Temptation. No, you should have called me the moment you got into trouble. Dammit, Garrek!"

"I'm not in trouble!" Garrek yelled back. Then he clenched his teeth and shook his head. "I didn't do anything to get into trouble with the MAs, but I should have known it was going to go down like this."

"Like what? What's going on? They said you're AWOL."

"No. I received an approved-leave chit from my commanding officer. Look, I gotta go find Harper. I'll tell you all about it when I get back."

"Have you told Harper about this?"

Garrek was silent.

"Man, what are you doing? You're sleeping with her and lying to her? You're lying to your family. This isn't like you, Garrek," Gray said.

The disappointment in his voice was not only audible, but Garrek could swear he felt the waves of it flooding him at this very moment.

"I'm going to fix this. Just let me get to Harper. I just have to talk to her before—" Garrek paused because his call waiting was beeping.

He pulled the phone from his ear and looked at the screen. Cursing again, he put it back to his ear.

"Listen, I'll be back in Temptation in a couple of

hours. I'll come straight to your house. Just wait for me there."

"You need to get a lawyer, Garrek. Those MAs plan to stay in town until they pick you up."

Yeah, that's exactly what they would do.

"Meet me at the Adberry place. At one o'clock," he told Gray. "I'll be there at one and I'll tell you everything."

"I'll be there," Gray said. "Be careful on your way back, and Garrek?"

"Yeah?" he answered with a sigh.

"The time for secrets is over. If you care about Harper at all, the time to come clean is now. While you still have a chance."

Garrek hung up with Gray and immediately answered the other call. Something told him he might already be too late for Harper.

"Yes, Rochelle?" he answered.

"I told you to call me ASAP. You don't know what that means anymore?"

"When did you tell me that?" he asked, squeezing the bridge of his nose, because it seemed all the stress had piled up in that spot.

"I texted you about fifteen minutes ago."

Again, Garrek pulled the phone away from his ear. He saw the text she was referring to, and then he knew.

Harper's phone had been right next to his on the nightstand.

Harper wasn't outside waiting in the truck. He knew that without even going downstairs.

"I can't do this with you right now, Rochelle."

"If not now, when? You're the one who wanted this early paternity test and now you've got it," she said.

He had wanted the test. He'd wanted to know as soon as possible if the one night he'd gotten so drunk he couldn't see straight—let alone remind himself that sleeping with his captain's daughter was a terrible idea— had cost him his career. And made him a father.

"What did the test say?" he asked her tersely.

She was silent.

"Not in the mood for this, Rochelle! You've been playing games for months now. First telling your father that we were engaged, then changing that story to say I refused to answer your calls once you told me you were pregnant. I could lose my career over this!" he yelled.

Then Garrek forced himself to calm down. He knew that he wasn't innocent in this situation. Anger over the fact that Harper had probably seen that text message and run out on him was overruling his normally calm demeanor. Before coming to Temptation, he'd resigned himself to the fact that he was either going to be a father, or he was going to have to accept a reassignment because Captain Ainsley was never going to want him under his command after what had happened with Rochelle. And he wasn't certain he'd be promoted to any command post of his own. He'd thought he was fine with either scenario. Until Harper.

"It's not your baby, Garrek," she snapped. "Is that what you wanted to hear? I'm not carrying your baby."

Relief would have overwhelmed him if Garrek didn't know that time was still of the essence.

"Then get your father to call off the MAs he sent after me," he told her.

"He wouldn't do that. He told you to take leave until we got this straightened out. I was there in his office when he said it."

"So was I," he told her. "But MAs just knocked on my brother's door looking for me. Now you call your father and get this straight before I return to Washington."

"Good," she said with a sigh. "You're coming home. When can I expect you?"

The hopefulness in her voice was annoying. Just as the phone calls at insane hours of the night that had commenced after their one night together and the day she'd camped out in front of his house on the base had been. He'd told her the morning he woke up naked in her bed that it was a mistake. He was very clear about not wanting any type of relationship with her. Garrek had thought that had been reinforced by him not returning her calls or texts in the following weeks.

He'd been mistaken. His night with Rochelle had definitely turned into a fatal attraction—one that was now threatening to have him arrested.

# Chapter 14

It took Garrek two hours to get to a rental car facility, secure another car and then drive back to Temptation. All the time there was only one thought on his mind: getting to Harper.

He'd tried calling and texting her, to no avail. He'd slammed his palms against the steering wheel of the car, yelled at other drivers on the road and cursed his own foolishness. Now, as he turned onto the road leading to the Presley farm, he was rehearsing what he would say to her. None of it sounded like it would make a difference.

How was it that they'd come to be invested in each other so soon? He'd never thought this could happen to him. Never even considered that he would fall so hard for one woman, let alone so quickly. Didn't relationships take a long time to build? Real love a good amount of time to flourish? Maybe he wasn't in love with her after all.

Garrek knew that wasn't true. If it were, he wouldn't be parking the car and preparing to get out and face whatever was necessary to make her understand. He didn't see her truck, so Garrek checked his phone one more time. He'd turned the volume all the way up just in case she called him back while he was on the highway with the windows down to let in the light breeze today. Nothing, he realized with a heavy sigh.

Sticking the phone in his pocket, Garrek grabbed his keys and stepped out of the car. He headed up the steps of the Presley house and knocked on the door.

Arnold appeared.

"Half an hour earlier and I would have been watching those MAs arrest you," he said before Garrek could even speak.

Garrek bit back a curse and shook his head. "It's not what you think," he told the older man.

Arnold gave him a brief nod. "You've got ten minutes to come in here and tell me what I should be thinking about this situation."

When he stepped aside, Garrek walked into the house. Linus wasn't there, which was a relief. It was going to be hard enough explaining this to the father of the woman he'd slept with last night. Having her grandfather there, too, might have required Garrek have a firearm for protection.

"I made a mistake," Garrek began. "I was drunk one night and I slept with my captain's daughter. She took the one night to mean something more. I told her it wasn't. Repeatedly. Then she said she was pregnant. Before I could react, my captain was calling me into his office.

He gave me a leave chit to figure out what I was going to do—marry his daughter or find a new career. I came here to figure it out."

"And my daughter," Arnold began tightly. "*She* was how you were going to figure out what to do about your unborn child and disgracing everything the navy taught you?"

He was taller than Garrek by a couple of inches, with broad shoulders and thick hands. An eagle, anchor, globe—honor, courage and commitment—Marine Corps tattoo peeked from beneath the short shirtsleeve on his left bicep. His face was affixed in a scowl, hands fisted.

Garrek stood tall, legs slightly separated, hands relaxed at his sides. He held eye contact and spoke in a clear and undeterred voice. "Harper had nothing to do with this. She was unexpected, and I never meant for any of this to touch her," he told Arnold.

"And how did you think this was all going to play out? You get one woman pregnant and run away. Then you come here and start doing the same irresponsible things with a new woman. And don't you dare try to hide behind your family troubles. You're a grown man. I expect you to act like one, even when you're under the gun," Arnold said sternly.

He sounded like an angry father, something Garrek had never had the opportunity to hear in his lifetime. The times he'd seen his father had been so short and far between that Theodor wasn't given any chance to speak angrily at any of his children.

"Yes, sir," Garrek replied. "I understand your irritation at this situation. I can only reiterate that this was not my intention. Things just began happening between

Harper and myself, and I should have said something sooner. I know that now."

"You're damn right you should have said something sooner. You stood right in my kitchen and told me there was nothing I needed to know about your position in the military."

There'd been nothing Garrek had wanted to tell Arnold or Linus Presley yesterday morning. Now he wished that he could go back and redo the past.

"I just need to see Harper, sir. I really need to talk to her," he said. "I know you're angry with me and that I'm probably the last person in the world you want near your daughter. And I can understand that. Really, I can. But I need to see her. If she tells me to go, I will. But not until I see her, not until I try to explain."

For endless moments, it seemed, Arnold simply stared at him. Probably trying to figure out which was the easiest way to kill him. Garrek didn't care. At this moment he didn't give a damn if the MAs circled back to find him here. He just needed to see Harper first.

"She's not here," Arnold told him. "Hasn't been here all night. I thought that meant she was with you."

Garrek cursed. "She was."

"Then where is she now?"

"I don't know," he answered and turned to head toward the door. "But I'm going to find her."

"You'd better hope you do, before the MAs find you," Arnold said. "Garrek."

He stopped at the door and turned back to look at Harper's father.

"This is gonna hurt her. You're the first man I've seen my ladybug with, so I know you mean something to her. You swore to me you wouldn't hurt her. But you did," he told him solemnly.

"I know, sir. And I'm so sorry for that. I'm going to try to fix it. I am," Garrek said and then left the house.

He climbed back into his car and tried to think of anywhere she would go, because nothing else mattered to him now. Not his career in the navy, not Rochelle, Captain Ainsley, the Adberry house or his father's money.

There was nothing without her.

"I can't do anything without talking to her first," Garrek said as he stood in one of the front rooms of the Adberry house.

He'd been there for about fifteen minutes now, telling Gray everything that had happened in Washington.

"You need an attorney," Gray said. "I called Phil, my lawyer, while I was waiting for you. He doesn't handle these types of cases, but he can put us in touch with someone familiar with military law. If your captain approved your leave, but then sent the MAs after you, he's gotta be in some type of violation. You definitely need representation before you think about going back to Washington."

"I'll go back and I'll face whatever I have to there. But not until I see Harper," he said earnestly.

"She hasn't called you back since she left the hotel?" Gray asked him.

Garrek shook his head. "I know she saw that text message from Rochelle. It's the only thing that makes any sense."

"That sucks," Gray said and shook his head. "But you know what else I'm going to say."

"I don't need you to say it," Garrek snapped, cutting him off. "I know I should have told her sooner. I just didn't think we were going to end up here. I didn't know I was going to be in a position to owe her an explanation."

"And what makes you think you are now?"

"Because I can't breathe, Gray!" he yelled. "Standing here trying to tell you what's going on while I'm worried sick about where she might be and what she's probably thinking is constricting my chest as if a boulder were sitting on it. I want to punch something or someone. I want to yell in frustration over all the rum and Cokes I had that night, over the stupid condom that broke and the woman who couldn't get it through her head that I was never going to marry her!"

Gray clapped a hand on Garrek's shoulder. "Slow down. It's going to be all right," he said. "She's gotta be around here somewhere. When I told Morgan what was going on, she sent Harper a text."

"What?" Gray asked. "Did she reply to Morgan? What did she say?"

"Just that she had to pick up the tile and that the master bathroom would be finished tomorrow," Gray told him.

Then Gray was right. She was back in Temptation and she was all right. Or rather, she was physically okay. Emotionally, Garrek believed she was probably a mess. If she were feeling anything like he was at this moment, a mess would be an understatement.

"You gotta get yourself together before you see her," Gray told him.

Garrek nodded just as his phone rang.

He hurriedly pulled it from his pocket and answered without looking at the caller ID. It was Gen.

"Hey. Why didn't you tell me?" she asked immediately. "Gray said you were in some kind of trouble."

Garrek looked over to his brother and frowned.

"Hey, Gen," Garrek said, and Gray shrugged as if he hadn't done anything wrong.

"I'm not in trouble," Garrek told her.

"Military police are looking for you, Garrek. That sounds like trouble."

"I can handle it."

"Sure. Just like you've been handling it so far."

"I got this, Gen. Trust me."

"No," she said adamantly. "That's what's wrong with us now. We all have trust issues. And don't deny it. If we knew how to trust each other, you wouldn't have kept this a secret from the people who care most about you. Now Gray said he contacted an attorney for you. I'm switching things around on my schedule so I'll be able to meet you in Washington when you get there."

"Wait a minute," Garrek protested. "I don't need you coming to Washington. I can handle this."

"Whatever," she replied as if he hadn't said a word. "Tell Gray I'll be there when he gets there with you. And when I see you—after I hug you—I'm slapping you for making me worry. I told Gemma I'd get one in for her, too."

Oh, damn, she'd called Gemma.

"You're lucky she can't get away to come, or she'd be right there, too. I'll see you soon. Love you, big bro."

He clenched his teeth, hating the fact that this crappy feeling seemed to be settling over him comfortably.

"Love you, little sis," he said before disconnecting the call.

A few seconds later, he turned to see Gray leaning against the doorjamb.

"I can't believe you told on me," he said.

"Why? Because I'm the oldest and you're used to everybody running to me to snitch?" Gray chuckled. "Well, since we're all adults now, I figured it was good to start sharing the wealth."

Garrek managed a small smile. He did appreciate his siblings. He hadn't realized how much until this very moment. They were ready to rally behind him, even though he'd kept all this from them. They had his back, just like their mother had made them promise they would. Garrek wasn't sure anyone even cared about upholding Olivia's oath anymore. Since their father's death, Garrek hadn't been sure about anything where the Taylors were concerned. Now he was certain that his siblings would stand by him until the end, whenever that turned out to be.

Garrek only wished Harper would still be willing to do the same.

Pat's Bar and Grille was located on the corner of Bailey and Linden Streets, about six blocks away from city hall. It was a red-shingled two-story building with green windowpanes and a big light-up sign hanging from the second-story window, reading Pat's. On the Linden Street side, an addition had been built three years ago to add more seating. Strands of Christmas lights hung around the border. On the Bailey Street side were more Christmas lights and a cartoon image of Patricia Ann Rhinehart, the bar's founder, standing close to a grill with a beer mug in her hand, painted on the window.

The last time Harper had been here was for Jill Langston's bridal shower a year ago. Jill had dated Marlon for a year while they were all in high school. If not for her and Jill being members of the debate team, Harper probably would not have been invited to the shower or the wedding. She didn't usually drink or socialize, for that matter, so it felt a little foreign to take a seat at the end of the bar and ask for a martini. It was the drink her aunt Laura preferred, so Harper had tasted it at her house many times before.

Aunt Laura, who had immediately sensed something was wrong when Harper showed up at her house to drop the tiles off with Marlon earlier this afternoon.

"You all right, Harps?" she'd asked.

When Harper had said she was fine, Laura Jane Hilton Presley had taken her by the chin and stared at her.

"You're not fine," her aunt stated. "What happened?"

It would have been normal for Harper to insist she was okay and go off to lick her wounds alone. She'd done that all of her life. This time it felt dishonest, just like Garrek had been with her.

"I tried it and it didn't work," Harper said.

She'd moved away from her aunt then, going to stand near the fireplace in their living room. Framed pictures lined the mantel—the one of Aunt Laura and Uncle Giff on their wedding day caught Harper's eye. They looked so young. Uncle Giff's hair was thick and black, in contrast to the thinning, predominantly gray it was now. Aunt Laura's hair was long, curly and blond, her blue eyes sparkling with laughter. Now she wore her hair chin length. The pair also looked as if they were madly in love, which was similar to how they still acted thirty-two years later.

"Why didn't it work with Garrek?" her aunt asked.

Harper shrugged, not even bothering to ask how Aunt Laura knew exactly who and what she was referring to. Everybody in town had been talking about her and Garrek since the night he'd placed that bid on her.

"He lied to me," Harper said, still too embarrassed to turn around. "I asked him if he was involved with someone and he said no."

"And now you've learned that he is?" Laura asked.

"Yes," Harper replied. If she closed her eyes, she could still see the message on his phone screen. So she didn't close her eyes. But it didn't matter; the pain was still as sharp.

"How did you find out?"

She frowned and ran her finger along a frame that held a picture of her and her grandfather.

"I read his text message." Harper sighed. "I know I shouldn't have, and it wasn't intentional. But he wasn't going to tell me. He was just going to continue lying until he left town."

"So he's going back into the service?" Laura asked.

"I don't know. I guess. I don't know anything about him, Aunt Laura. How can I feel so betrayed and so hurt over somebody I barely know?"

"Because your heart knows," Laura said. "Sometimes it works that way. The heart leads, and then everything else follows. Did you ask him about the text message?"

Harper shook her head. She sat down on the couch and let her head fall back, closing her eyes even though she knew exactly what she'd see when she did.

"I just left," she said.

"But you feel like he owes you an explanation?"

"No," Harper said. "I don't want to see him. I feel like

he should have told me, and I'm pissed that he didn't.
But I didn't want to ask him about it. I didn't want to—"

Her aunt had come to sit beside her, placing a hand
over Harper's. "Were you more afraid of him telling you
that you were wrong about the message? Or of confirm-
ing that he'd really lied to you?"

Harper didn't have a chance to answer, because Marlon and Craig had come into the room talking about the
tile mix-up. She'd left a half hour later and driven around
until finally ending up here at Pat's.

The bartender had just delivered her drink and a ten-
tative smile when Harper's momentary solitude was interrupted.

"I'll have a vodka on the rocks, Jimmy," Leah said
as she dropped her Michael Kors clutch on the bar top
and sat on the stool next to Harper.

"Drinking alone?" she asked. "Never mind, don't answer that. I already know."

Harper decided today was a good day to ignore Leah.
She didn't have much interest in what the woman had to
say on a regular day, and right at this moment she could
not have cared less. So she picked up her glass, took a
sip and continued to stare up at the television. There was
a baseball game on, but Harper was just as uninterested
in who was playing or winning as she was in Leah.

However, the batter who had just struck out reminded
her of little Jack when he'd been learning to hit a ball
with his first baseball bat. Harper's heart warmed at the
thought. She'd loved that day at the lake. Even though it
was unexpected, it had turned out to be a really fun day.
It was also the first time that she'd thought she could be
falling for Garrek.

It had happened so quickly, starting with the way he'd

held Lily in his arms and talked to both the little girl and her doll. He'd explained to Susie, the doll, why it was important to listen to her mommy, and Lily had looked elated. Then he'd pitched the ball super slowly to Jack numerous times until Jack finally got a hit. After that, Garrek had celebrated with his nephew as if he were already a baseball pro.

His interactions with the twins endeared him to her in a way that Harper hadn't expected. Since she'd never thought of having her own children, it never occurred to her to pay attention to the way a man interacted with kids. Yet the entire time they were at the lake, she'd watched Garrek. From how he wiped Jack's mouth after he'd eaten a piece of lemon meringue pie—because he'd gotten most of it on his face—to his adorable confusion when Lily asked him to retwist her hair and clip her barrette on the end.

That night Harper had known genuine trepidation. She'd already had sexy dreams about this man. Then he'd saved her life and followed that with a searing first kiss. The picnic had simply plucked away another layer of her resistance. Those first warning feelings should have been, she thought now, a sign of the disastrous end.

"I guess you would come here to drown your misery after all that's been going on today."

Harper hadn't been paying any attention to Leah, hoping that would make the pain-in-the-butt woman leave. It hadn't.

"I'm not drowning anything in misery," Harper replied. "Just having a drink."

"Right," Leah said, nodding at Jimmy the bartender and then drumming her too-long and too-pink nails on the bar.

The sound was annoying, and Harper sighed heavily.

"Look, you don't have to try to pretend with me. If I were banging a guy who didn't have the sense to wrap it up to prevent getting his captain's daughter pregnant, I'd need a drink, too."

All the air drained from Harper's lungs, and she turned slowly to face Leah.

"What did you just say?"

"Oh, come on, Harper. That innocent act you toss around town is getting so old. I know you've seen those fine MAs walking around today. They've been talking to everybody about Garrek Taylor and the trouble he's in. They even went to see your daddy. You know, after I told them that Garrek had moved on to...well, to you."

The last was said with a smirk.

But Harper was too busy replaying all the words the annoying woman had just spoken to notice.

"The masters-at-arms," she said, hearing the words and hating the sound. "They're looking for Garrek."

"Of course they are, Harper. That's what happens when you go AWOL," Leah chided.

Harper gulped from her glass and set it back on the bar with a thump. Neither Aunt Laura nor Marlon and Craig had mentioned anyone coming to their house to look for Garrek. Their house was a little farther out than the farm, so maybe the MAs hadn't gotten there yet.

"Look," Leah continued. "I don't know if there's a punishment for being stupid, but if there were, you'd deserve it. What were you thinking, jumping into bed with a guy like that? You should have known he was out of your league, even if he did turn out to be a jerk. Now you have the entire town talking about how he paid all that money at the auction to sleep with you, just months after he got some other poor girl pregnant."

Harper was going to be sick. She felt dizzy and warm and she knew she needed to get home before she embarrassed herself…again. But not before she attempted to verify Leah's story.

"Who told you he got someone pregnant? The MAs wouldn't divulge that type of information to civilians," Harper said.

"Well, if you need all the dirt I certainly won't hold back," Leah snapped. "Rusty Baines was going into the gym just as I was coming out. You know he's always had a thing for me. I gave him a chance once, but he didn't cut it. And I swear, he has the hardest head in the world. Just keeps finding any reason to talk to me now. Anyway, Rusty immediately starts talking about the MAs hanging around town. He said his grandfather knew one of the MAs' daddy from the navy. So he called him up, and that's how he got the scoop about the captain's daughter."

Harper wanted to scream. Wasn't anything private anymore?

She slipped off the stool and reached in her back pocket for some bills she then tossed on the bar.

"Where you going?" Leah asked. "He's probably long gone. You know those military folk are relentless. They probably have Garrek cuffed and in the back of their shiny black car by now."

Harper was already walking away, leaving Leah to shout after her.

"Get a spine, Harper!" Leah yelled when Harper reached for the door handle. "Say good riddance to that loser and go back to your dull and boring life with that hammer and nail!"

She was going to leave. It was what she needed to do, really it was. But not this time. Harper just couldn't do it this time.

She walked back to the bar where Leah sat, grabbing a bottle from one of the tables on her way. Harper had no idea what was in the bottle. And before she could think better of the act, she was tipping that bottle over Leah's head, watching as the red wine flattened the fresh curls on Leah's head, down her carefully made up face and onto the tight white blouse she wore.

"If this is the only way to shut you up," Harper said. "I guess I'll have to oblige you. Again."

When the bottle was empty Harper set it on the bar and tossed some more money over to pay for it. Then she walked out of Pat's with her heart thumping wildly and her mind circling around the fact that Garrek had not been the man she'd thought he was. She didn't know who he was or why she'd ever gotten involved with him. All she knew right now was that regret, mixed with that sickly emotion called love, was a bitter pill to swallow.

## Chapter 15

It was close to ten that night when Garrek finally saw headlights coming up the road. Two hours ago he'd finally given up the hope of Harper calling or texting him. And since Morgan had sworn to him that she hadn't heard from Harper again since the earlier text, Garrek knew there was only one other option.

He'd parked his second rental car about a mile down the road beneath some trees and walked back to where he now stood beside the barn on the Presley farm. The first few minutes he'd stood there, he'd felt foolish. Now, hours later, after seeing the headlights, he felt hopeful.

Tomorrow he would be leaving to head back to Washington. Gray was going with him, and his attorney was going to meet them at the airport, where Gray's private jet would be waiting. Captain Ainsley was out of line with the AWOL accusation, and Garrek wasn't about to take that lying down. He'd worked too hard for too long to get where he was, and he wouldn't let a momentary lapse in judgment destroy him.

As for Harper, well, he didn't think he'd worked hard enough where she was concerned. And for that he was profoundly sorry. He hoped against all else that she would let him remedy that situation. If not, Garrek would do exactly as he'd told Arnold he would. He would leave her alone. He respected her and himself enough to walk away without any further incident, if that was what Harper truly wanted.

She drove right past the barn in her truck, and Garrek immediately stood from the front porch steps where he'd been waiting for her. The instant their gazes locked Garrek knew this was worse than he could have ever imagined. Her eyes were full of hurt while the determined way in which she approached spoke of anger.

"Can we talk?" he asked when what he really wanted to do was go to her and pull her into his arms.

But touching her right now didn't seem like a good idea, especially since she was already shaking her head as she stopped just short of the steps.

"I don't think—"

"Please," he said, interrupting her. "Just to talk."

She seemed to think about it before nodding and Garrek breathed a sigh of relief. He walked down the steps and stood in front of her. She instantly backed away, the pain in her eyes palpable. He cringed inwardly.

Garrek began walking toward the barn, because at this point that was all he could do. He opened the door and waited while she walked inside. As he closed the door, he noticed that she'd turned on the lights but remained standing near the doors. He tried not to recall the last time they were in this space, because it only made him feel worse about what was going on now.

"First, I need you to know that I never meant to hurt you," he stated.

"Let's just start with what your true intention was when you came here, Garrek," she said. "Remember, I asked you that question when we were at the Adberry house, and you said it was because your father left you that property."

"That was the reason I came to Temptation," he said and then held up a hand so she wouldn't interrupt him. "I could have gone anywhere, Harper. Anywhere in the US to get away from my situation in Washington. My captain granted me a leave chit, and I thought it made sense to take the time to deal with the issues surrounding my father and his death."

She looked at him like that explanation didn't change one bit the way she thought about him at this moment. Garrek continued.

"I slept with Rochelle Ainsley one night after a group dinner and way too many drinks. The condom broke. The next morning I made it perfectly clear to Rochelle that our night together was a mistake. I apologized to her and moved on. Five weeks ago, I was scheduled to ship out for two years, taking a new post as department head. Three days before the ship-out date, Rochelle told me she was pregnant. I was called into my captain's office, and he told me I had to figure out what to do about honoring his daughter and the commitment I made to her by sleeping with her. He gave me some time, which I took to think."

She crossed her arms over her chest, tilting her head

as if she were growing tired of his words. Garrek continued anyway.

"That first night I came to Temptation, I just wanted a drink and to go to bed. I was tired from driving and wanted to finally clear my head."

"You probably should have taken a hint from the party on the base and cut down your drinking," she said.

"You're right," he said with a nod. "But I do not regret the misunderstanding that took place that night. No, I did not walk into that hall intending to bid on a date with a woman I didn't know. But looking back on that night, I realize that was a pivotal moment in my life. It was as if it were meant to happen exactly the way it did to get us to this point right now."

"Forgive me if I'd rather not be standing in a barn, a few feet away from someone who thought so little of me that he couldn't even tell me the truth," she said. "You had so many opportunities, Garrek. I didn't push. I respected your privacy, because I had secrets of my own. But the moment things shifted between us, I wanted to know more about what happened on the base and why you were here. How long you were staying. All of it! I asked and you lied!" Her arms fell to her sides as she took a step toward him.

"I was scared!" he shouted back, and then clamped his lips shut.

She did not speak but blinked rapidly, as if his outburst had startled her. It had shocked him. This was not the way he usually acted. Then again, he wasn't usually fighting for something as important as she'd grown to be to him.

"I didn't really know what was happening between us," he began again, his tone quiet even though his heart was thumping wildly. "I couldn't understand why it was so hard to stay away from you, to not touch you, not want you. I'd been so sure about what I wanted my life to be and how I expected it to play out before. I just wasn't prepared for you."

His words seemed to echo in the huge space as she stared off toward the tractor. Garrek ran a hand down the back of his head.

"So is it your baby?" she asked.

"No. It's not."

"If you were granted a leave chit, why are the MAs here looking for you?"

"I don't know. But I'm leaving tomorrow to get it all figured out."

"You're leaving?" she asked and immediately looked up at him.

"Yes," he said, searching her face for any clue that she might want him to stay. There was none. "That's why I needed to see you tonight. I couldn't go without explaining to you."

She started to nod. "Oh, right. Yes. You're going back to Washington."

"This wasn't what I planned," he started.

"Stop saying that!" she yelled and pushed her fingers through her hair. "Nobody can plan every aspect of their life, Garrek. Do you think I planned to have some drunk idiot at a frat party attack me?"

Anger simmered in him instantly. "This is not the same."

"It's not that different," she continued. "We both got into situations that quickly spiraled out of control. I ran away from mine, you ran away from yours. The difference is, I told you. When I thought we were at a point where honesty needed to override my fear, I told you what happened to me. You backed away again. That seems to be your preference."

He took a step toward her because not touching her was threatening his sanity. She took a step away and then pulled on the barn door before looking over to him. "Thanks for the explanation. I hope you get everything straightened out when you return to Washington."

"Harper," he said, not sure what to say next.

"You have a life to live," she continued. "Hopefully it turns out to be the one you planned. As for me, I'll move on. I did it before, I can do it again. Goodbye, Garrek."

She stepped out of the barn, and he started to follow her. But Harper turned quickly, holding up a hand to stop him this time.

"Don't. This is finished. You said what you needed to say. I listened. Now we both go our separate ways and do the things we need to do to survive this episode. That's how life works, Garrek. The give-and-take while the world continues to spin around us. We keep going. That's it."

When she turned away from him this time, Garrek remained still. He watched her until he saw her close the front door of the house behind her. The sound of it slamming echoed in his mind and caused a thump in his chest.

She was gone and she was right—they needed to keep moving. He had things to do, a situation to fix. But as Garrek walked to his car he realized, now more than ever, that Harper was still mistaken about one thing: they weren't meant to go their separate ways. He'd been at that hall, raising his hand for another drink at the exact moment he was supposed to be. That silly auction was meant to serve a purpose, and even if nobody else cared at this point, Garrek was listening. He was hearing and believing and ready to reach out for the future that he felt deep down in his soul was meant for him.

Yes, Garrek had believed there was a plan for his life, and now there was no doubt in his mind that the plan was never his to make. He wasn't about to miss the blessing that he knew Harper was meant to be to him by walking away and never looking back—like his parents had done, because they never took the chance on coming back to each other. He was going to Washington in the morning, but then he was coming back for Harper.

No matter what, he was coming back to Temptation for her.

## Chapter 16

Four weeks later, Harper ended a call with her contact at the American Program Bureau. With a smile of contentment, she sat back on the front steps of the Adberry house.

It was nearing ten o'clock on a Friday morning. The sky was a brilliant blue, sun beaming on an eighty-nine-degree day. She wore cutoff jeans and an old T-shirt, tennis shoes on her feet and a white bandanna wrapped around her head to hold her hair back. They'd finally finished demolition on parts of the house and she had the new permits from the county and the historical society tucked safely in her briefcase. Work would begin on the restoration of the house as soon as Craig, who was serving as project manager on this job, and the rest of the crew arrived.

Beginning the first week of October, she would be

traveling to four universities across the state of Virginia, speaking to incoming freshmen about sexual assault.

One week after Harper had returned from the impromptu trip to Richmond, she'd decided it was time to really let go of her past. The only way she could do that was by talking about it. Still a little nervous about her father and grandfather's reactions, especially on the heels of everything that had gone down with Garrek, she'd decided to tell Morgan and Wendy first. The two ladies had been a steady support in those days right after Garrek left Temptation, even though Harper had sworn she hadn't needed any assistance in moving on. After years of having no close friends, it had just become easier to not lean on anyone and deal all on her own. This time, Morgan and Wendy had made sure she knew that she didn't have to go that route.

"You are not a coward," Morgan had insisted after Harper had gone through the entire story about Len and the frat party again.

They'd been in Morgan's sitting room. Her doctor had put her on bed rest the day after Garrek and Gray had left for Washington, so Ms. Ida Mae had temporarily moved into one of the newly remodeled guest rooms in Morgan and Gray's house. The sitting room had been Morgan's idea as an extension of the master bedroom. She had been lying on the chaise lounge—which was the only other location, other than her bed, where she had permission to be.

Wendy had been sitting sideways in one of the highback antique chairs across from Morgan, her legs over one arm. Harper had been pacing the rose-colored area rug as she'd talked.

"Absolutely not," Wendy added. "You're a boss for

beating him down the way you did. I bet he thought twice about harassing any other girl after his nose was busted."

Harper had to smile at that. "I don't know. I looked him up, though. He's coaching at a North Carolina college now. He has a wife and a daughter."

She didn't know why she'd tracked Len down—she'd only known that she'd wanted to know what he'd made of his life since she'd basically given him a pass to move on without any consequences for what he'd done to her. Harper had been thinking a lot about that in the days since she'd told Garrek.

"Because he was never punished, he probably never thought he did anything wrong," Morgan said. "What a shame."

"I don't really care," Harper said. "He can have his family and his job, it doesn't matter to me. What matters more is that no other young lady has to endure the torture I've put myself through these past years. If I could just warn them."

"That's a great idea," Morgan had said. "You could speak at college campuses. Share your story and let them know it's okay to talk about this issue."

From there the idea had been planted, and Harper had been diligently researching and talking to people to figure out how she could make this happen. She hadn't pressed charges against Len all those years ago, and she realized now that she should have. But instead of trying to go against the statute of limitations and possibly press for a civil trial, Harper wanted to make it more about the other women who might fall prey to this same situation. So she planned to tell her story to any and all of the college students who would listen, in the hopes that she could get even one person to come forward after an assault happened to them, or, the better scenario, that she could prevent another young lady from having to deal with this issue at all.

So her smile today was one of triumph. After talking to Morgan and Wendy, she'd invited Uncle Giff and Aunt Laura and the boys over to the farm for dinner. While they were enjoying the strawberry shortcake that Harper had made because it was Pops's favorite, she told them her story. The men in her family were all ready to go to North Carolina and find Len Ruffin, but Aunt Laura saw the bigger picture. She saw the woman this incident had made Harper. That had made Harper feel good, and had solidified her resolve to talk to others about her story.

Now, the first speaking engagements were set via a national representative company that had agreed to work with her, even though she wasn't a celebrity and had no other viable platform. In this instance, being a survivor was enough.

Harper felt accomplished this morning. She was ready to start work on the house and ready to make her mark on this world. She was winning.

And then her phone chimed with an email.

Harper opened the message and read it, wondering what to think of the words.

In the weeks that Garrek had been gone, she'd heard from him at least once a day. At first the text messages were nerve-racking, as she was trying to forget what they'd shared. But when each of Garrek's messages spoke of the Adberry house and the plans to bring it back to its former glory, Harper began to slip into her comfort zone. She was the company he'd hired to do a service. That was all.

Opening his emails had become part of her daily routine—only today's words instantly threw her off kilter.

Please meet me at Adberry House, 7 p.m. tonight.

Was Garrek back in Temptation? If so, why hadn't anyone told her?

She'd sat up on the steps then, her hands shaking slightly as she held the phone and continued to stare down at it. There was no need for her to be nervous or anxious. This was business, she reminded herself. Of course he was going to come back when he knew she was about to start work on the house. That made sense.

The butterflies that seemed to be awakened by the message and the warmth that was already beginning to spread throughout her body did not make sense, because what she and Garrek had had was over. Harper was certain of that.

Garrek was running late.

His flight had been delayed, and one of the back tires on the rental car had gone flat when he was just half an hour away from the airport. So he'd called the rental company and had them meet him with another car. Then there was an accident on the highway, so his hour-long drive to Temptation had taken an hour and forty-five minutes.

Now, finally, he used the key Gray had given him to his house to let himself in at almost three o'clock Friday afternoon. Gray was also due home today after a business trip to Miami. Garrek felt bad about taking Gray away from his family a month ago when he'd had to return to Washington. He'd tried to get Gray to stay here, but his brother had insisted. As it turned out, it was good having him there. Garrek hadn't realized how much he missed having people in his corner all these years. But Gray and Gen were adamant about staying in Washington until he was cleared of any wrongdoing. And the lawyer Gray hired for him, Justin Marcone, a former marine, had been fantastic. Within hours after they'd arrived on base, demanding to speak to Captain Ainsley directly, the commander's ploy to bend Garrek to his will had come crumbling down.

"MAs showed up at the home of Grayson Taylor looking for Lieutenant Commander Garrek Taylor twenty-four hours ago. I'll be representing Lieutenant Commander Taylor and would like to see the civilian custody and court order," Justin had told the officer sitting at the desk outside Captain Ainsley's office.

The young woman had looked perplexed and immediately gone into Captain Ainsley's office. Minutes later the tall man with almond skin with snow-white hair and beard appeared. Garrek had immediately stood at attention for William Ainsley, the man who had been a mentor to him for the past five years.

"Come into my office," Ainsley had grumbled.

At his command Garrek had walked behind Justin into the captain's office. Per Justin's instructions, Gray and Gen had stayed at the hotel where they'd checked in prior to Justin and Garrek making their way to the base.

The office door had closed, and Garrek and Justin were both invited to take a seat. Garrek hadn't spoken to Rochelle since earlier the day before, so he had no idea what, if anything, she'd told her father. Rochelle had lied to her father before, telling him that she and Garrek had been in a relationship until she announced she was pregnant. That had been the beginning of this nightmare, so Garrek didn't put it past her to lie again. Only this time, he was ready. He'd insisted Rochelle give him the name and address for the facility that conducted the prenatal testing. She'd countered that he could simply use the kit they provided to submit his DNA, but Garrek had told her he wanted to go in person, and he had.

So when he called for a copy of the report to be faxed to him before he'd even boarded the plane to Washington, there had been no resistance. By the time they'd arrived at the hotel, the test results were waiting for him. And now they were safely tucked in the front breast pocket of his suit.

"Do you have the required paperwork for my review?" Justin had asked once they had been seated for a few silent moments.

"He knows what this is about," the captain said. "There was no need for outside involvement."

"The outside involvement, as I understand, Captain Ainsley, were the MAs who were sent to look for my client. My client whom you gave authorized leave, as evidenced by this signed and documented form," Justin said as he opened his briefcase and pulled out a copy.

The captain didn't even look at the paperwork that Justin slid onto his desk. Instead he continued to stare at Garrek.

"She's my only child. My daughter, my soul, since her mother's death ten years ago," he told Garrek.

Garrek was about to speak, but a glance in Justin's direction had him remaining silent.

"I told you to get your head together, to come back here and do the right thing. But that's not what you did."

"Captain Ainsley, I'm going to have to insist you provide the necessary documentation—"

"You don't get to insist anything here, young man," the captain had replied quickly and harshly to Justin. "You weren't holding up your end of the deal, Taylor." He'd turned his attention back to Garrek and now stood up slowly, flattening his palms on the desk. "I helped train you. I recommended you for that detail, and in three more years you would have been captain, with your own squadron. You would have made me proud."

"I never would have married your daughter," Garrek told him, because he knew that's what the man really wanted.

In all fairness, Garrek could think of it now as William Ainsley wanting his daughter to be happy. To have stability and a family in the military similar to the one her father had supplied for Rochelle and her mother. He could look Ainsley in the eye and admit that he understood that thought process more now than he had when he'd left here a month ago. He owed that to Arnold and Linus Presley and to the woman who had opened his eyes to what his life could be like.

"I was never in love with her," Garrek continued. "I've apologized for the misunderstanding between Rochelle and me before. I won't do it again."

"You will do as I say, Lieutenant! You will be a man and take responsibility!" Ainsley continued.

Justin stood at that moment.

"I'm going to assume that the lack of proper paperwork means this matter is void," he said.

Ainsley's head looked as if it were about to snap as he turned to glare at Justin. "There is no paperwork!" he yelled. "I ordered those plebs to go to that rustic old town and find my pilot. They were to bring him back and we would have handled this in house, the way it's supposed to be."

Justin nodded as if he'd known all along that something shady like this was going on. Since Garrek had the leave slip with the required signatures on it giving him permission to be on extended leave, they both knew the AWOL claim was bogus. Still, they'd had to approach everything from a legal standpoint to keep Garrek's job.

"In that case, Captain," Justin said with just the barest hint of a grin, "your commanding officer will receive a letter from my office within five days demanding your resignation for abuse of power and whatever other charges I can come up with. Good day to you, sir."

Justin had looked at Garrek as he'd headed to the door. Garrek stood to follow him. He reached into his jacket pocket and pulled out the piece of paper with the test results. Dropping it on the desk, he looked at Captain Ainsley again.

"These are the results from the prenatal DNA test. I'm not the father of Rochelle's baby. I have four more years on my commission, and I'll be asking to be reassigned so I can serve them out. Up until the night I made a terrible misjudgment, it had been an honor to serve with you," Garrek told him before leaving.

The next weeks had been filled with more interviews and meetings, and finally Garrek received a new commission after the official announcement that Captain William Ainsley would be retiring from the US Navy.

Now, Garrek was back in Temptation to take care of one last bit of business before preparing to ship out at the end of next week.

"Who is that coming in here?"

Garrek heard the question just as he dropped his bag near the door. Gray and Morgan knew he was coming in today, and they both had insisted that he stay with them this time. Garrek hadn't argued, because in the month that he'd been away, he'd missed his niece and nephew more than he thought was possible. He'd only missed one other person more than them, which was another reason he was so irritated about being late.

"Hey, Ms. Ida Mae. It's me, Garrek," he said as he stepped into the parlor to see Morgan's grandmother standing in the middle of the floor, two wet towels in hand and a dry one tossed over her shoulder.

"What's going on?" Garrek asked her.

Ida Mae breathed a sigh of relief. "Thank God somebody got here in time. I thought I was gonna have to deliver those twins on my own."

"What?" Garrek asked about two seconds before he heard a deep moan.

They both raced to the hallway just as Morgan came to stand at the top of the stairs.

"I need a ride to the hospital," she said and then grabbed the bottom of her stomach and moaned once more.

# Chapter 17

"It's only August. They're not supposed to be here yet!" Morgan yelled from the passenger seat of Garrek's car.

"Told you before, babies work on their own time. Doctors don't know everything," Ms. Ida Mae chimed in from the back seat.

"But they're the doctors!" Morgan yelled again and gripped the door handle until her knuckles turned white. The other hand had reached across the console to grasp Garrek's arm.

She moaned and yanked on his arm, and the car swerved as her action caught Garrek off guard.

"Oh, Lawd, we may all need the doctor by the time we make it to the hospital," Ms. Ida Mae commented.

Garrek frowned at her in the rearview mirror. Not because of her nonstop commentary since he'd arrived at the house, but because she was still carrying those towels like she really thought she was going to need them.

"Just keep breathing," Garrek said, because that's the only thing he knew to say to a pregnant woman who looked as if she were about to do bodily harm if somebody didn't hurry and get those babies out of her.

Morgan nodded. "I am. I am," she said.

Garrek nodded and breathed, too. His heart was thumping wildly as he tried to remember his way to the hospital and think of how else he could help Morgan get through this.

"Did you call Gray?" she asked as she lay back on the headrest. Her tone between contractions was rather subdued, in Garrek's opinion, but he would gladly take that in lieu of the nails in his arm and deep moaning.

"Yeah, he was just leaving the airport," Garrek told her. "And Wendy said she's picking up the twins from camp and will head straight to the hospital."

Morgan nodded at his words, and two seconds later she let out a moan and pressed back in the seat as if she were about to spread her legs and push.

"Turn left here!" Ms. Ida Mae screamed. "Just pull up at the ER entrance and open the door, I'll do the rest."

Garrek didn't like the sound of that. But sure enough, as soon as he pulled up in front of the double set of glass doors, the back door of the car opened and Ida Mae jumped out. She opened Morgan's door and made quick work of the seat belt Garrek had had to struggle to get around Morgan's girth while she'd been digging her fingers into his back through a contraction.

"Lady having two babies over here!" Ida Mae was yelling to two nurses who were clearly on their smoke break.

Garrek had gotten out of the car by then and was looking for a wheelchair as he stepped onto the sidewalk. He saw none and ran to the glass doors to see if anyone was around whom he could ask for help, because the nurses on break were still smoking. That was, until Ida Mae leaned Morgan against the car and marched over to them.

"Didn't you hear what I said?" she asked with both hands propped on her slim hips. "My granddaughter is about to have twins, and if either one of them falls out on this sidewalk because you two simpletons are too busy over here smoking, I'm gonna get a switch and start whuppin' some behinds!"

The women moved faster than Garrek even thought they could. One of them ran past him into the hospital while he went to join the other as she tried to assist Morgan. They'd only taken a couple of steps when the first nurse came through the doors with the wheelchair.

"That's more like it," Ida Mae was saying as she pushed her glasses up onto her face.

Garrek helped Morgan into the wheelchair, looking into her strained face once more.

"It'll be okay now," he said. "We're at the hospital. The doctors will take good care of you."

Half an hour later, Garrek wasn't so sure of those words.

Morgan lay in a hospital bed surrounded by white sheets and beeping machines, her pain more intense than ever. Wendy was there now and she'd taken a position on Morgan's left, holding her hand as she squeezed. Ida Mae sat in the waiting room with Jack and Lily, because she said she didn't want the children to see Morgan in such pain, but Garrek thought differently. He'd noted the usually calm and decisive Ida Mae Bonet had been frazzled and on edge since he'd arrived at the house.

His guess was she didn't like seeing her granddaughter in pain, either.

Garrek had to admit it wasn't something he'd ever imagined witnessing, but here he was. He'd promised Gray that he wouldn't leave Morgan's side until he got here, so no matter how uncomfortable this was making him feel, he was going to stay.

"What's that noise?" he asked during a rare moment when Morgan wasn't moaning.

"It's the babies' heartbeats," Wendy answered. "You can see their heart rates right here."

She'd been wiping Morgan's forehead with a damp cloth, but she nodded in the direction of a machine that was spitting out white tape. Garrek moved closer, lifting the tape to see two sets of squiggly black lines.

"Are they all right?" he asked, because Wendy was a nurse. She also seemed pretty calm, so he figured that must mean she knew what was going on.

"Yes. They're doing fine. Their heart rates are steady."

"But she's in so much pain."

Wendy gave him a calming smile and a nod. "Yeah, that's typically how this works."

"I can't take it," Garrek said.

"Most men can't," Wendy replied. "But this should be good practice for you. I'm sure you'll have your own babies one day."

Garrek shook his head. "I don't know."

"Oh, I know," Wendy said. "Trust me."

He was just about to ask her what she meant when the door opened. Garrek expected to see another nurse or possibly one of the doctors, but he was surprised to see Harper instead.

"Hey," she said, coming in and going straight to the side of the bed where Wendy stood. "I got your text. How's she doing?"

Morgan moaned as if on cue, and Harper touched a hand to her stomach.

Garrek looked down to see Harper's hand moving over the protruding mound and felt something tighten in his chest.

"She's hanging in there," Wendy said. "Especially since her brother-in-law swooped in like a knight in shining armor to save her from Granny."

Harper looked up at him then. She slowly pulled her hand away from Morgan's stomach when she realized that's what he'd been staring at, and backed away from the bed.

"I didn't know you were here," she said to him and then gave Wendy an I'll-deal-with-you-later look.

"Didn't you get my email?" he asked.

"He sent you an email?" Wendy asked.

Morgan moaned again, squeezing Wendy's hand until her sister had to lean over the bed.

"Yes. I did," Harper replied, this time not looking at or answering Wendy.

"Why did you come back?" she asked. "I mean, are you checking on the house? Because we haven't really started anything yet. I thought I told you that in the email earlier this week."

Morgan's contraction had apparently passed, because Wendy could now stand up straight. She used her free hand to wipe Morgan's forehead while looking back to Harper and asking, "You emailed him earlier this week?"

"Yes. I did," Garrek replied to Harper's questions.

"But there was something else I needed to discuss with you, and I felt it would be better received face-to-face."

"Hot damn, face-to-face! Now that's what I'm talking about. No more of that email crap!" Wendy added, her excitement clear.

This time when Morgan grabbed Wendy's hand, it was before she said, "Leave them alone."

Garrek leaned in then and kissed his sister-in-law on the cheek. He desperately wanted to be alone with Harper, but he couldn't, because Gray walked in the second Garrek was thinking about him. And not a moment too soon, because Morgan didn't moan with the next contraction. This time she screamed as if somebody were doing bodily harm to her. Garrek figured that was kind of true.

He stepped back from the bed and let Gray take his place beside his wife, while Wendy began focusing all of her attention on Morgan.

"You think we should go now?" Garrek said just as two more nurses came into the room.

Harper didn't look like she particularly wanted to go with him, but she did glance back at Morgan, who was writhing on the bed now and nodded to him.

"No!" Morgan yelled. "Stay! I want you both here."

"She's ready to start pushing," one of the nurses said.

"I'll get Dr. Savani," the other one said and moved to the door. "If you're staying, you need to stand over this way. As long as this birth goes naturally, you'll be fine over here. If things start to change, we'll have to take her back for a C-section."

Garrek had no idea what the woman was talking about, but Harper did. When she reached for his hand and pulled him over toward the door where the nurse told them to stand, Garrek went willingly. He also held on to her hand until the moment his new niece and nephew were born.

Six hours later, when Emma Olivia and Ryan Theodor Taylor were sleeping soundly in the All Saints Hospital nursery, Garrek stood on the front porch of the Adberry house.

It was well past the time he'd asked her to meet him here, but Harper could see that the time change hadn't caused too much of a problem. He'd changed since they'd left the hospital, which made her extremely glad she'd decided to do the same.

He wore black slacks and a white polo shirt, and she'd taken off the awful shorts and T-shirt she'd been wearing at the hospital and put on a white sundress that had been a treat to herself after enduring endless weeks of Wendy's harassing her to upgrade her wardrobe. Harper had also pulled her hair back into a ponytail and put on strappy black sandals. As she walked up the front steps and Garrek stared intently at her, she figured the outfit had been a good choice.

"Hi," she said when they were standing just a few feet from each other.

"Hi," he replied. "Thank you for agreeing to come. I know you were tired from being at the hospital all that time."

She nodded. "Yeah, I've never witnessed childbirth up close and personal before." And it was more intense than she could have possibly imagined. Intense and totally breathtaking.

"Me either," he said with a chuckle.

They stood for a few awkward moments, the sun having already set and the night steadily creeping in. There was a slight breeze, and the smell of summer and magnolias drifted through the air.

"You look really nice," he said then.

He'd slipped his hands into the front pockets of his slacks and stood in that way that made her feel like running up and throwing her arms around him. It was a simple feeling that Harper had decided to allow herself. Since receiving that email from him this morning, she'd been volleying back and forth with how she felt about seeing him again after all they'd been through. Her final thought—which hadn't come until the moment Morgan had the new twins—was that she and Garrek really hadn't gone through that much.

Sure, their meeting had been out of the ordinary, and the resulting times they'd spent together could be construed as a very physical beginning, and the end—well, as endings went, Harper was certain theirs had been pretty civil.

"Thanks," she said. "I'm more comfortable in jeans."

"You look great in jeans, too," he said, and the calm she'd been fighting for vanished.

Those butterflies were back, flitting around in her stomach as if they hadn't been MIA for the last month.

"You look good, too," she admitted. "Four weeks' worth of good."

He smiled, and she really did want to run to him. It was silly, she knew, but she'd missed him. She'd been angry and hurt because he hadn't trusted her enough to be honest with her, but being without him had been worse.

"It's been a really long four weeks," he said and then took a step toward her.

Her fingers moved at her sides as she thought about touching him again, but he stopped as if catching himself.

"Why don't you come inside," he said, quickly turning away from her.

Harper wondered why they needed to go inside. She knew what was in there—partially gutted rooms, a staircase with no railing, lots of dust and some supplies. Monday morning was going to be an even bigger day than today had turned out to be. But she followed him anyway, gasping when she saw all the candles. There were two on each step leading all the way up, to equal forty-four, as she knew exactly how many steps were on the grand staircase. On the bottom step was a bottle of champagne and two glasses.

"Are we celebrating something?" she asked nervously.

"I hope so," he replied and reached for her hand.

For a moment Harper could only stare at it. She wasn't sure what was happening here or how she should feel about it. What she knew for certain was that she wasn't going to let fear rule her. Not this time. Not ever again.

She took Garrek's hand.

He led her closer to the steps and turned her to face him, taking her other hand in his.

"In three weeks I'll be leaving for my next assignment," he said.

"Oh" was all Harper could manage.

"I have four more years left on my commission, but I was able to work out a teaching assignment in Pensacola, instead of heading back out to sea."

Harper nodded. "Okay." Pensacola wasn't Temptation.

"There are a couple of things I want to have in place before I go."

His hands were warm on hers, and she gulped as he took a step closer to her.

"I want to make sure the house restoration is getting off to a good start."

A part of her sank. A huge wanting, needing part of her. She blinked and then remembered that he was speaking to her, so she nodded and cleared her throat. "Well, we got some things done today before I received the text from Wendy. But Monday we'll get started early, and as long as the supplies we've ordered arrive on time and there are no big weather delays, we should come in right around our seven- to eight-week projection."

"Good," he said. "That's really good."

They were silent then. Harper was uncomfortable.

"Okay," she told him. "Well, if that's all you wanted to talk to me about, I'll just get going."

She attempted to walk away, but Garrek held on to her hands.

"Harper." He said her name quietly.

"Yes, Garrek," she replied.

"I wasn't sure," he began and then stopped.

"You weren't sure about what?"

"When this first started…all of this…" he said and looked around. "I just wasn't sure. Now, I know without a doubt that I want to be wherever you are. Every minute that I can, every second, I just want to be with you."

Harper was speechless. She'd thought—well, hell, she hadn't known what to think.

"I know it was rocky in the beginning, but I'd like to start over. I'd like to take you on a real date. I'd planned one for tonight, but the babies came."

She managed a smile. "Yeah, the babies."

"And then I thought about canceling, but no, this is too important. You are too important."

He was rubbing his thumbs over the backs of her

hands, and it was driving Harper crazy because she wanted to hug him. She wanted to feel him close to her, holding her tightly.

"It'll be long-distance for a while, but I'll get leave again and then we can be together. I know I'm not really good at the relationship thing, but I want to try. I want us to try. I want to marry you, but I know it's too soon. I know you need more. You told me so. Dates and courting, that's what my mother would have called it. You need all of that."

She was already shaking her head and finally pulling her hands out of his.

"No, Garrek, I don't need any of that. I only need you," she said and then closed the small distance between them.

Finally, she wrapped her arms around his neck and pulled him close. "I just need you, secrets and all. Just you, Garrek."

His arms slid around her waist and he held her tight, just right.

"Kiss me," she whispered.

"I love you," he replied.

"I love you," she said softly, just seconds before his lips touched hers and then again when he pulled back slightly. "I love you, too."

\* \* \* \* \*

## COMING NEXT MONTH
### Available April 17, 2018

### #569 IT MUST BE LOVE
*The Chandler Legacy* • by Nicki Night

Jewel Chandler's list of boyfriend requirements is extensive—and Sterling Bishop doesn't meet any of them. Sure, the wealthy businessman is gorgeous, but he also has an ex-wife and a young daughter. When steamy days melt into desire-fueled nights, Jewel wonders if he's truly the one for her.

### #570 A SAN DIEGO ROMANCE
*Millionaire Moguls* • by Kianna Alexander

Christopher Marland, president of Millionaire Moguls of San Diego, is too busy for a personal life. When Eliza Ellicott arrives back in town, he knows no woman has ever compared. A broken heart gave Eliza the drive to succeed, and she's opened a new boutique. Can she trust him again?

### #571 RETURN TO ME
*The DuGrandpres of Charleston* • by Jacquelin Thomas

Austin DuGrandpre never had a relationship with his father. Determined that his son—put up for adoption without his knowledge—won't suffer the same fate, he tracks him to the home of Bree Collins. The all-consuming attraction is unexpected, but when Bree learns Austin's true motives she faces potential heartbreak.

### #572 WINNING HER HEART
*Bay Point Confessions* • by Harmony Evans

Celebrity chef Micah Langston's ambition keeps him successful and single. He plans to open a restaurant in his hometown—and that means checking out the competition. Jasmine Kennedy is falling for Micah until she discovers his new venture will ruin her grandmother's business. Has betrayal spoiled her appetite for love?

KPCNM0418